The main room was ~~~~~~ ~~~~ ~~~ into the doorway for a bre~~ ~~ ~~esn air. A murmur of male voices came from outside, on the front steps.

'They say,' she heard, 'he dunno where that typhoid's a comin' frum. Always thought he was a likely young feller m'self, but seems as though a doctor that knowed his job would of found out about that typhoid long ago.'

A cold sick feeling clutched at the pit of Sue's stomach and prickled her scalp.

'That's so,' came a second voice. 'Take a thing like that to show a body up. Guess likely he's all right for cuts an' pimples, but no doctor at all's better'n a bum one. Feller like that's a danger to the community.'

Sue didn't wait to hear any more, but turned and fled back into the hall. Bill was still talking, his dark head bent in interested and friendly attention. Sue wanted to scream.

Helen Dore Boylston

Sue Barton – Rural Nurse

KNIGHT BOOKS
Hodder and Stoughton

First published in Great Britain by
The Bodley Head Ltd in 1942

This edition first published by Knight Books in 1967

Tenth impression 1980

―――――――――――――――――

Set, printed and bound in Great Britain for
Hodder and Stoughton Paperbacks, a
division of Hodder and Stoughton Ltd.,
Mill Road, Dunton Green, Sevenoaks,
Kent (Editorial Office: 47 Bedford
Square, London, WC1 3DP) by
Cox & Wyman Ltd., Reading

ISBN 0 340 04007 6

Contents

For my Mother, Mabel M. Boylston

I

'It's awful bad luck-'

THE room was bright with lamplight, gay with orange curtains, and pleasantly fragrant with the smell of bath powder. It was also phenomenally untidy. A wardrobe trunk partly blocked the doorway into the hall. Hatboxes and shoes were strewn over the floor. A suitcase lay open on the bed, surrounded by piles of clothing, and the chairs were buried under mounds of assorted underwear and blue uniform dresses.

An underground train rumbling up from lower Manhattan shook the bedroom windows with a brief fury, and, in the stillness that followed its passing, noises in the tiny house were very distinct. Upstairs, off the square hallway between the two bedrooms, there was a gurgling of water, and the faint rustle of silk. Downstairs, footsteps hurried back and forth, dishes clinked, and a girl's voice with a markedly Canadian accent announced, 'There! That ought to be enough, Marianna, even if they all come.'

A younger voice, slightly nasal, replied, 'Sure – I guess so – unless there's a lot of husbands. Men eat sump'n fierce.'

'There won't be many – only two or three, I should think – and the police, of course.'

'*Cops!* Hey! What is this – a party for members of the underworld?'

'Not unless all the Henry Street nurses but me are leading double lives. Anyway, your "cops" are only Sergeant O'Day. You couldn't have a farewell party for Sue without him. She adores him.'

'Oh! *I* know – he's the guy rescued her from that drunk in the tenement.' There was a pause. Then, 'Gee, Kit, I – I can't hardly believe Sue's going off to get married. It – it's goin' to be kind of awful round here with her gone, ain't – isn't it?'

7

'Quite!' said the other voice briefly, and added, 'but after all, it isn't as if we wouldn't be seeing her. If Bill can get me that job in the Winslow Hospital, and you come with me to go into training, we'll only be about fifty miles from where they'll be living.'

'Yeah, I know. But all the same –'

'Goodness!' said Kit, changing the subject hastily. 'What *is* Sue doing? There hasn't been a sound for ages.'

'Bath, I guess.'

'Still?' Kit raised her voice. 'Shall we go up and drag her out, or just leave her there to receive the guests in the bathroom?'

'You needn't bother to yell,' said a clear voice suddenly from upstairs. 'I can hear you perfectly. Besides, I'm –'

'Oh yes! We know. You're out of the tub – at least, one hand is – and that makes you practically ready.'

'Not at all! I –'

A crash of dishes and a wail from Marianna ended the conversation.

Upstairs, a slender girl with damply curling red hair emerged from the bathroom, shrugging on a dressing-gown as she came. At the threshold of the bedroom the untidiness halted her for an instant in dismay. Then she stepped briskly over the litter on the floor and, arriving at the dressing-table by a devious route, began to brush her hair. It gleamed, copper-red and gold, under the strokes of the brush.

The face reflected in the mirror was an intensely alive face – the eyes steady beneath level brows, the nose delicate, the round but obstinate chin offset by a humorous, sensitive mouth.

Sue Barton looked at herself critically, changing the brush to her left hand, and smiling as the mirror caught the sparkle of a diamond on her third finger. Was it only three weeks ago that she had been so wretched about Bill and their broken engagement – only two weeks ago that she had been lying in bed, ill with a cold, and had opened her eyes to see Bill standing in the doorway? Marianna had brought that about – the little monkey!

'Golly!' Sue thought. 'All my bright ideas about leading my own life certainly took a running jump into the lake – in less than half a second!'

Her resignation from the Henry Street Visiting Nurse Service had been a wrench, all the same. She had loved her work at Henry Street. But once she had given in – had relinquished her long and determined effort to cling to her independence – her approaching marriage had overshadowed everything else. 'Nobody can say I'm not one-track,' she told Kit the day after her resignation. 'Now I'm really started up the aisle, I'm practically the world's champion sprinter!'

'Well, why not?' Katherine Van Dyke said. 'You've had Bill dangling for three years. You broke your engagement because he mentioned that he was sick of waiting and –'

'You mean, because he started being take-it-or-leave-it!'

Sue grinned at her image in the mirror, remembering the argument which had resulted from that remark. Then, hearing a sound of light steps mounting the stairs, she glanced up to see a tall girl in the doorway – a square-shouldered girl with intelligent brown eyes, an impertinent, upturned nose, and arched slim eyebrows that seemed perpetually amused.

'For heaven's sake, Sue!' Kit began. 'Aren't you dressed yet? They'll be here in another min –' She broke off, to stare appalled at the confusion in the room. 'What happened?' she said. 'Did you have an attack of epilepsy – or was it just Marianna helping?'

'Marianna. Nice, isn't it?'

Kit grinned. 'And she thinks she's going to be a nurse! Golly, what *do* you suppose will happen to her in a hospital?'

'Oh, don't worry about Marianna. It's the hospital I'm praying for. All the same, Kit, she's a lot better than she was when she came, and she's really trying. I haven't heard her say "Geeze" in a month.'

'That was getting her to go to night school. It was the smartest thing you ever did, Miss Barton. Mercy! Will you *ever* forget the way she was – a first-class little shop-lifter – at eighteen –'

'And talking out of the corner of her mouth – and sullen and defiant and –'

They smiled at each other, recalling the overwhelming Marianna who had broken into their kitchen that snowy night a year ago – a dirty, furious Marianna, child of the New York streets, hiding terror and gratitude behind a façade of bluster.

'Come on, Sue! Do hurry,' Kit said, returning to the present.

'I am. You wouldn't like to do something for me, would you?'

'Depends on what it is,' said Kit, instantly suspicious.

'*Da*rling! You're so impulsive! I always say there's nothing like really old friends! They –'

'If it's clear up this mess – the answer is NO!'

'That's that, then,' said Sue cheerfully, brushing at a tangle of red curls.

Kit leaned against the dressing-table, her face suddenly wistful. 'Well,' she said lightly, after a moment, 'tomorrow night at this time you'll be home in New Hampshire, in the bosom of your family – and a month from now you'll be in Springdale as Dr. William Barry's brand-new wife.'

Sue, glancing up, saw a shadow in the brown eyes and looked away quickly.

'They dew say,' Kit went on in what she imagined to be New Hampshire hill dialect, 'that that Mrs. Barry's hair ain't nacheral. And have you *seen* the way she keeps house?'

'Here! Nobody in New Hampshire was ever guilty of that accent!'

'All right! Have it your own way. Bill found out about his typhoids yet?'

'No. The whole thing's queer – because they've practically stamped out typhoid over the whole State.' Sue discarded her dressing-gown and disappeared into the cupboard, her scanty undies a momentary shimmer of pink. 'I'll tell you about it later.'

'Decided where you're going on your honeymoon?'

'Oh, just somewhere in Bill's car – South if I have anything to say about it – because it's bad enough to be getting married in February and to spend a draughty winter in the White Mountains without freezing to death on your honeymoon, too – *Gosh!*' The exclamation was shocked and startled. Kit's eyes widened.

'What is it?'

'My – engagement ring! I've lost it!'

Kit reached the cupboard in two strides to find Sue on her hands and knees.

'But it must be there, Sue! It can't just take off for parts unknown!'

She looked up. 'It was the oddest thing. I was hunting for the belt to my blue dress – sort of pawing around, you know. The ring caught on something – I felt it – and pulled off.'

'Well, if you will break your engagement and pine away like a dear old-fashioned girl, you can't expect things to fit you. Anyway, don't worry. Go on and dress. I'll look for it.'

Sue remained where she was. 'It just doesn't make sense. The ring was a bit loose, but it wasn't as loose as all that.'

'Never mind, old thing. I'll find it.' Kit stepped out into the hall. 'Marianna!' she shouted. 'Be a lamb and bring a torch, will you? Sue's lost her engagement ring.'

A robust young figure bounded up the stairs, wiry golden-brown hair standing out at all angles, incongruous above the tailored simplicity of a dark blue dress and neat white collar and cuffs – selected by Kit.

'Gee!' Marianna exploded into the room. 'That's terrible! It – it's awful bad luck to lose an engagement ring. Because even if you find it again it means –' Kit's furious glare stopped her.

'Where did you get notions like that, Marianna?'

'Aw, my aunt – she used to tell me.'

'Why should you have faith in your aunt's superstitions when you hadn't a bit of faith in anything else about her? You

said yourself that she was stupid and cruel. She let you live
with her after your parents died – just so she could put you to
work and take the money. She lied and stole. She beat you – and
you hated her so you ran away. Now you pop up with this sudden, touching belief in her. Why?'

'Well, things used to come out like she said they would, lots
of times.'

Sue interrupted from the interior of the cupboard. 'How
about helping me a little?' she said.

'Sorry,' said Marianna. 'You dress and we'll look.'

Sue dressed worriedly while the girls searched for the ring.
It was not on the cupboard floor, nor caught on any of the remaining garments, and the search was still going on when the
doorbell rang.

'Oh, heavens! There they are!' Kit said, scrambling to her
feet. 'I'll go. We can look some more later. Hurry up, Sue!'

'No!' said Sue quietly. 'You go. I am staying here until I
find that ring!'

Kit stared at her. 'But Sue – you *can't*! The party's for you!
You have to be there when people come.'

Sue's jaw set forward. 'I'm sorry, Kitten,' she said. 'But
after all, that ring meant a lot of hard work for Bill. I –'

'I know, darling, but it isn't going to fly away. You can come
back later and look for it.'

'I can stay and look, too.'

The bell rang again – more sharply this time.

'Oh!' Kit wailed and fled.

'It's all right, Sue,' Marianna said. 'Come on down. I guess
you do have to. I'll be back and look for it. I've just got one
more thing to do in the kitchen. An' if I don't find the ring
in a little while, then *you* try. But I *will* find it – honest! It
must be here!'

Sue considered for a long moment. 'All right,' she gave in at
last, unhappily, and turned to the door. Marianna followed her
downstairs and the little room was left to its untidiness.

Frost crystals crept delicately up the window-panes and the

opening of the front door upon voices and laughter sent a fluff of lint scurrying under the bed. The lamp, forgotten by Marianna, who was the last one to leave, shone cheerfully on Sue's tumbled belongings.

On the dressing-table were two enlarged snapshots in plain leather frames – one a picture of a family group, in which Sue stood laughing up into the face of a white-haired man whose likeness to her was as unmistakable as his professional appearance. Sue's mother had once remarked with a sigh, 'You can tell when a doctor *is* a doctor even in his sleep – they have the look, somehow. . . .' Mrs. Barton stood beside her husband in the picture, a plump dignified little woman, her eyes upon the tall boy who was Sue's brother, Ted. The other snapshot was of a young man in the white uniform of a hospital interne. He was tall and broad-shouldered, with a fine head and deep-set eyes which held the glint of a grave smile. Scrawled across the bottom of the snapshot were the words: 'Yours, Bill,' and a date of two years ago.

An open drawer of the wardrobe trunk revealed a portion of a grey sleeve – the uniform of the student nurses in the great hospital in which Sue had received her nurse's training. She and Kit, and Constance Halliday, their closest friend, had come to the hospital the same day, though from very different parts of the country. Sue came from New Hampshire, but this had nothing whatever to do with the fact that the tall young doctor of the snapshot was now practising in the town of Springdale in that State. The practice was offered him and he took it. That was all; but it was very pleasant for Sue, since she was about to become his wife.

Kit had come to the hospital from Canada, and Connie from Chicago. The three had been inseparable from the first moment of their meeting, going gaily from one scrape to another. The training had been more difficult for Connie than for Sue and Kit, for Connie was the daughter of a very rich man and the school as a whole regarded her with suspicion, doubting her seriousness or her ability to stick to her training. Connie, however, *had* stuck to it, and it was during her last year of training that Philip Saunders, a spectacled and entirely strange young man, had fallen down the underground steps on top of her. They were married shortly after Connie's graduation.

Sue and Kit, bereft of their 'third half', had continued on together, in the Visiting Nurse Service at Henry Street, in New York, missing Connie deeply, and more homesick for the hospital and old times than they ever admitted, in spite of their enthusiasm for Henry Street.

Sue's trunk held further reminders of those days – garments old and shabby now. On the rack in one side of the trunk was the dressing-gown Sue had worn in the hospital ward when she was recovering from an appendix operation. A darn on the shoulder of the dressing-gown was the only trace left of the terrible night when Sue had struggled to prevent a delirious patient from strangling the night nurse in an attempt to escape. Beside the dressing-gown hung a winter coat – second-best by this time – which Sue had wrapped round her to keep her teeth from chattering with cold – and fright – the night she lay hidden under the supervisor's bed. And next to it was the dress in which Sue had gone to Connie's wedding in the Little Church round the Corner, only last summer – the same dress which had seen the beginning of real trouble with Bill.

On the chair were the blue Henry Street uniforms, starched and crisp and clean-smelling – as if they had never been in dark tenements rank with the odours of cabbage, onions, herring, and humanity. Sue planned to wear those uniforms again after she was married, but this time on the winding roads of the White Mountains in a smell of wind and pine needles, and in lonely farmhouses, winter-white, or baking under the summer sun. The uniforms were still good, for they had been in use only a year, and that year had left few traces upon them except for a tiny snag on one sleeve cuff, made on a day when Sue had managed to prevent a lorry-driver from bleeding to death. The snag was inconspicuous, and had been made by a broken soda-water bottle, the contents of which had been used to wash the man's pumping wound.

A green chiffon evening dress hung from the cupboard door, and it, too, had a history, for Sue had worn it to a New York night club – with Bill – when he came on to be best man at Connie's wedding. He and Sue had had their final quarrel that night, had broken their engagement, and Bill's dazed eyes had watched the soft chiffon of that dress going away from him among the tables – Sue's red head a furious flame above it.

Just beyond the dress, in the gloom of the cupboard, was Sue's best winter coat, in the pocket of which nestled the lost ring, its fire blanketed by darkness.

Marianna found it there when she came back.

She came quickly up the stairs, flushed with her effort to speak correct English, and sighing in gusty relief as she closed the door behind her. She went straight to the cupboard and removed the clothes methodically, one by one, shaking them over the bed and then dropping them, with complete lack of method, on the floor. When the ring fell out of the coat pocket she snatched it up with an exclamation which would have horrified Sue, and took a step towards the door. Then she paused, looking soberly round the room, and presently sat down on the bed.

It would be *her* bed after tonight. There would be no more sleeping on the living-room couch. She would have a real bedroom, all her own. But Sue would be gone – and it was Sue who mattered more than anything in the world to Marianna. It had been Sue, that night a year ago, who had said that Marianna must stay with them and not sleep in cellars and doorways any more. It was Sue who had found Marianna an adequate job in a mail-order store, and it was for her sake that Marianna had given in at last about going to night school – because she wanted to be a nurse, like Sue.

As Marianna remembered these things, her jaw quivered. She rose abruptly to her feet. 'Bawl baby!' she said fiercely, and strode out of the room.

Chatter and laughter rose to meet her and Marianna confronted it stiffly, searching for Sue's red head among the guests, the ring clutched tightly in her hand. There was a crowd round the table on which the buffet supper had been set out, and the few husbands present, grateful for something to do with suddenly large hands, were filling plates for wives and friends of wives. Over by the french windows that opened on the tiny garden — bleak now, under the January moon — stood Sergeant O'Day, enormous in civilian clothes. His Irish eyes twinkled down at Sue and his deep voice boomed above the chatter.

Marianna made her way towards them, unaware of the interested glances of the nurses, who knew her story. Sue's ring was a tiny hardness in her hand. She paused behind Sue, waiting for an opportunity to speak.

'So ye're lavin' me for a handsomer man,' the Sergeant was saying. ' 'Tis missin' ye I'll be — th' red currls av ye blazin' amongst thim grey tenements an' yer pretty face poppin' out o' alleyways, wid a sthring av childher along, like th' tail to a kite.'

'If I'd known sooner that you felt this way,' said Sue gravely, 'I'd never in this world have left. Wild horses couldn't have dragged me from your side.'

The Sergeant beamed. 'There 'tis!' he roared, delighted. 'Blarneyin' an ould man into thinkin' he's a lad! 'Tis in luck yer young doctor will be, th' day, though he is takin' ye so far off. Is he a counthry boy?'

'No. He's spent most of his life in the city.'

'Save us! Then phwat's he doin' up in thim mountains?'

'Well, you see, he thinks there are too many doctors in the city and not enough in the country. He — he likes people, awfully. In a country practice you get closer to them, somehow. And anyway, he thinks you get more experience in a small community, as a general practitioner.'

' 'Tis serious, he is?'

'Very. Too serious, I think, sometimes — but sweet.'

'Well, I wish ye clear skies all th' way.' He dropped his voice slightly. 'If ye don't mind me askin' – have ye a raft of in-laws to make up to?'

Marianna stirred impatiently, deliberately breathing down Sue's neck.

'No,' said Sue. 'His mother isn't living. His father is a college professor, and there's a younger brother – a cripple from infantile paralysis – who's very brilliant. I've never met them because Bill's father has been teaching abroad – in one of those exchange professorship things – and Eliot is with him. But they'll be back next summer, for good.'

'Ah! Then ye'll not have much –'

The determined Marianna broke in. 'Sue! *Look!*' She held out her hand, palm up.

The ring flashed as Sue caught it up and slipped it on her finger. 'You *darling*, Marianna! *Where was it?*'

'In your coat pocket.'

Sergeant O'Day leaned forward. 'Phwat's all this? Did ye lose yer engagement ring?'

'Yes, I did – but not for long, thanks to Marianna.'

The big man's face sobered. 'Have a care, me gurrl,' he said slowly. ' 'Tis a warnin', maybe.'

'That just what I said!' Marianna put in.

Sue laughed, though she had a second of something oddly like fright. Everybody, she thought gloomily, was working overtime to give her bad luck. 'Don't tell me you're superstitious, too, Sergeant O'Day! It's bad enough to have Marianna croaking around, tying funeral wreaths on everything and tacking up coffin plates.'

'Don't ye talk so!' said the Sergeant sharply, and then reddened, grinning a little sheepishly. 'No matter. Maybe I don't belave it whan I use me head. Here, gurrl – yer friends is afther wantin' ye! Somethin' goes on.'

There was a general stir round the room and all eyes were turned to Sue.

'What –' she began, bewildered.

'Gwan wid ye – right up front where they can see ye.' The Sergeant propelled her forward into the centre of the room, where she found herself face to face with Miss Firrell, Henry Street's young Director of Nursing Education. Laughing groups round them moved back, leaving a cleared space. People who were sitting down stood up, and people who had been standing up decided to sit. Miss Firrell waited until the scraping of chairs and shuffling of feet subsided. Then she smiled at Sue and began to speak.

'I expect,' she said, 'that Miss Barton has been congratulated almost to the point of saturation on her coming marriage, so I won't go into that again. I'm sure she knows how much happiness we all wish for her –'

There was instant, hearty applause, and Sue flushed. She was recovering, however, from her first shock of surprise and stood waiting gravely. She looked less than her twenty-three years and almost fragile, standing there in the circle of faces – her red hair and smoke-blue dress uniting to emphasize her white skin and slender figure.

When the applause had died away Miss Firrell continued.

'I think most nurses have a weakness for adventure, especially when it is connected with their work, and while we are more than sorry to lose Miss Barton, I suspect that we all envy her the chance to do real pioneer nursing. It is also very gratifying to realize that the standards and traditions of Henry Street are expanding over the country, carried by our own nurses.'

She paused again and turned directly to Sue.

'We can't go with you, Miss Barton, much as we'd like to, but we *have* thought of a way in which we can all have a small share in your new work.' She reached behind her and received from the hands of one of the nurses a large package done up in tissue paper. 'We hope, Miss Barton, that this gift will be useful to you for many years.'

'Th-thank you,' Sue stammered.

Marianna dashed forward with a small table and Sue put

the package on it. Then, while everyone watched with embarrassing attention, Sue unwrapped her gift.

The black pigskin sides of a beautiful new Henry Street bag emerged from the rustling paper and Sue gave a little gasp. Her initials, S.B., were marked on it in gold letters.

'Go on, open it,' Miss Firrell urged.

Sue opened it. The bag was fully equipped, each separate article bearing a little tag with the name of the nurse who gave it. Sue lifted the things out, one by one: thermometers, hypodermic set, rubber tubing, two Henry Street aprons, a beautiful set of instruments – scissors, forceps, haemostats – the trays for sterilizing, the white enamel cups, three hand towels marked with her name, bottles for medicine, alcohol, and soap solution, every one of which had been filled. There was even the familiar supply of cotton and bandages and paper napkins.

There could have been no better gift; for Sue, if she were to work with Bill, would need, above all else, a Henry Street bag.

The faces round her waited, expectant.

'I – I don't know how to thank you,' she began, and paused. Formal expression of thanks seemed inadequate. It would be better to say, however awkwardly, exactly what she felt. 'I – suppose,' she said, 'that I've been too excited to think ahead about what I'll need, but you've done it for me. I can't – tell you how glad I am to have the bag. I – it will become a part of me, I suppose – the way the other one did. I hated to turn it in. And I'm glad the girls I worked with have given me this one. I – thanks awfully!' she finished, feeling that she had made a mess of the whole thing.

There was an instant of silence. Sue's words had been brief, but they had been spoken with the warmth of utter sincerity. Every nurse present understood the significance of Sue's statement that the bag would become a part of her. They knew how one's arm grew accustomed to the bag's weight, until its absence was a kind of loneliness – its presence a security. They knew how the fastenings became as personal as the shape of one's own hand – how the tourniquets, the bottles, the instruments, all grew close and intimate with use. And Sue's remark that she was glad the girls she worked with had given her the bag did not seem a merely polite form of thanks. They had all known the depths and satisfactions of comradeship that has its roots in work – in being a part of something more important than any individual. And they understood that the gift of the tools of her work, from them, was more gratifying than it would have been from anyone else, for it must surely be an expression of professional respect as well as of friendship.

And so their silence was actually more of an appreciation than the ripple of applause which followed a moment later.

The presentation of the bag, however, marked the beginning of the end of the party. The hour was growing late and after a little there was a general move to go, with attendant confusion of tramping and laughter, searching for mislaid compacts, and sudden returns from the street for forgotten galoshes. Kit was outside on the front steps, calling out last good-byes, the door wide open behind her and the icy wind sweeping through the house. Marianna closed the door, muttering under her breath when it was instantly reopened by a young husband dashing back for his wife's gloves.

Sue, just recovering from a severe cold, had moved well back out of the draught and was saying good-bye to Sergeant O'Day.

'Ye're weary,' the big policeman said gently. 'I'll not be afther kapin' ye.'

Sue looked up at him. Here was another good friend who was going out of her life. She was closing all the doors behind her.

'*Don't* go!' she said abruptly.

He understood.

'Now then,' he said. 'Nothin' stays put in this world. Ye must go eyther forrard or back.'

'I know. I'm sorry. I just had an off moment of being a shrinking little violet clinging to its flowerpot and not wanting to go out and grow in the ground, if you follow me. Though I don't know that anybody has ever accused New York of being a sheltering home for hothouse plants.' She gave him her hand. 'Good-bye, Sergeant O'Day, and thanks for knowing you.'

'Thanks yer own silf.' He looked down at the slender hand resting in his great paw. 'Seems a useless little thing,' he said, 'but 'taint. Good-bye, gurrl. I wish ye ivry happiness – and don't ye give heed to phwat I said o' y'r ring. 'Twas no warnin', surely, but a bit a' foolishness as crops up in me now an' agin. Good-bye to ye!'

His massive shoulders blocked the doorway for a moment. Then he was gone.

Sue remained where he had left her, feeling for her ring, turning it round and round on her finger. Kit, locking the front door, turned to glance at her.

'Goodness, Bat! You look all in. Why don't you go to bed?'

'You're so inspiring, dear – and so helpful. Where would I sleep – on the hall floor, or hanging from the chandelier?'

Marianna came out of the kitchen.

'I've cleared off your bed, Sue. You can get in it.'

'Thanks, old girl.' Sue moaned inwardly, knowing what Marianna's clearing off meant. 'I think I will, then, if nobody minds.' She moved slowly up the stairs. At the top she paused and looked down at them, Kit fine-boned and distinguished, Marianna tousled and robust. A lump rose in Sue's throat and suddenly, without a word, she smiled at them – a warm smile, unexpected and wholly charming. Then she went on, leaving them side by side and motionless.

'Aw, *geeze*!' Marianna said at last. Kit said nothing.

2

End and beginning

SUE was aware of the voice, but sleep held her inert. 'Hey! Sue!'
she heard again, dimly, and blinked as her eyes opened into a
shaft of winter sunlight. Then, from force of long habit, her
glance went to the clock on her bedside table and she sat bolt
upright. Five minutes to nine! She was late for duty!

'Wa-ait a minute!' said Marianna. 'You ain't goin' to work,
you're catchin' a train – and it don't go till two – but you gotta
finish packing.'

Sue relaxed. 'I forgot for a minute,' she said. 'But what are
you doing at home – oh yes!'

'Want me to write it down for you? You remember us – Kit
and me – we're havin' th' day off, specially to get you on the
train.'

Sue looked up at the tousled head and earnest face bending
over her, and smiled. She mustn't make a fuss about leaving the
girls. They'd be upset. It was so awful when a person stopped
acting like her familiar self. She pushed back the bedcovers and
stretched. 'Oooo!' she said. 'Thanks for shutting the window.'

Marianna grunted, and Kit's voice downstairs announced
briskly, 'You've got a letter, Sue – from Springdale.'

Sue was instantly wide awake.

'So nice to know it's in the house!' she called. 'But don't let
me hurry you, dear. I wouldn't want you to get all out of breath
rushing upstairs with it.'

Kit paused half-way up the staircase. 'Oh, well, in that case
I'll just rest here until you come.'

'Kit!' Sue shrieked. 'I hate you! Marianna – take it away
from her!'

Marianna grinned and folded her arms across the back of a
chair. She had never ceased to be fascinated by the light-hearted

banter between Sue and Kit; for until Marianna came to live with them all the 'back talk' she had known had been ugly, the result of hatred or fear, and a prelude to violence. She had never dreamed that two people could insult each other affectionately. She waited now, enchanted, for the next move.

Kit disappointed her, however, for after a moment's hesitation she came on up the stairs and handed the letter to Sue.

It was not from Bill!

Sue looked at the unfamiliar handwriting with sudden uneasiness. Who would write to her from Springdale except Bill – unless something had happened to him? Her mouth was dry as she tore off the end of the envelope and drew out the neatly folded pages, turning them hastily to look for the signature. Then her face cleared.

'Golly,' she said. 'I forgot all about her.'

'Who?' from Kit.

'Veazie Ann Cooney.'

'*Veazie* – you're making that up!'

'No, I'm not, honestly. She's Bill's housekeeper. He thought it would be nice if I wrote and asked her –' Sue's voice trailed off as she began to read.

The letter was headed 'Springdale, N.H., January 13th.'

DEAR MISS BARTON, – Thank you for your real nice letter asking me to stay on after you and the Dr. are married. I'll be glad to. I guess you and me will get along fine. You will need somebody if you're going right on working with the Dr. like he said.

Now I hope you will excuse me putting my oar in. My late husband always said I was a great hand to mind other folks' business. Nose trouble he called it, on account of being cranky the last years of his life. But I think seeing as you will be Mrs. Dr. Barry you ought to know about this. Things are not going very good here just now and the Dr. don't realize, being young and not used to country ways. It seems as though somebody has a spite against him. He don't think so and he don't do anything about it but he ought to. He says you are a small town girl yourself, so you will know that things like that once they get to going in a little place can end up pretty bad if they are not nipped in the bud first off and maybe you can make him see it. There have been windows broke in the surgery 2 or 3 times and once his tyres cut. Yesterday when he was visiting them two typhoids, he can't find out where they got it though I don't see what's the odds now they have it, somebody took and scratched the word QUACK in big high letters on the door of his car. It is enough to make a body boil after all he done for folks around here after everybody having to get along for years with Dr. Kendall when he was so old they had to prop him up while they were doing for him and anybody real sick had to depend on the Lord. You'd think now they got a real smart young doctor they'd be thankful. But no.

Please don't tell Dr. Barry I said anything, but I thought if you know you can kind of worm it out of him and make him pay some attention to it. I will close now wishing you every happiness. – Yrs truly,

VEAZIE ANN COONEY.

Sue had laughed aloud at portions of the letter, but her eyes returned to the words 'seems as though somebody has a spite against him'. Bill was foolish to ignore that – unless Mrs. Cooney was making a mountain out of a molehill. Perhaps it wasn't anything much. 'I'll talk to him,' she thought, and laughed again. 'Nose trouble!' she said aloud.

'Get you a handkerchief?' Kit inquired.

'No thanks,' absently. 'Here! Read this.' Sue pulled the covers back round her and sat hugging her knees.

Kit sat down on the foot of the bed and read the letter aloud. 'Well,' she said when she had finished. 'I should say your home life will be far from dull. Quite a gal, isn't she? But Sue, what do you think goes on?'

'I wouldn't know – but I'm going to find out. It may be

just silly kids trying to be funny – only I don't see kids thinking up exactly that kind of thing all by themselves. Anyway, I
can't do anything about it now.'

'No. It's funny about the typhoids, though.'

Marianna spoke suddenly.

'What's he tryin' to find out?'

'He wants to find out where they got it,' Sue explained.

'But I don't see what difference –'

'You and Veazie Ann Cooney! He's trying to prevent other
people getting it.'

'Well, what –'

'Look, Marianna – in order to get typhoid it has to be taken
into the alimentary tract – it has to be in something you eat or
drink. I mean, you don't ever get it by breathing it or just being
round where it is. But it has to start somewhere in food or
drink, and it's up to Bill to find out where. Personally I'd never
pick cold water or milk as an ideal place in which to raise a
large family, but typhoid bacilli simply adore it.'

'Yeah, but the people already got typhoid.'

'I know. But other people might get it from the same source,
and the next thing you know there's an epidemic.'

'Oh,' said Marianna with dignity.

'And,' Sue went on, 'Bill is having a perfectly impossible
time. There are two cases, both in the same family – a grandmother and a ten-year-old girl. Bill says the source of infection
must have been brought into the house because the grandmother never goes out. He's tested their well and found nothing. They get their milk from the local dairy, and he tested it,
too, and all the milkmen and drivers, in case there might be a
carrier.'

'What's a carrier?'

'A permanent Free Home for Typhoid Bacilli. I mean, it's
somebody who's had typhoid and recovered, but continues
to breed germs – without being ill any more. It's very rare,
actually.'

'But if it doesn't – doesn't – make them ill, I don't see –'

'Look,' said Sue patiently. 'If the infected person doesn't happen to be very clean he's likely to infect someone else. Of course, if you can keep him away from other people's food it's generally all right, but –'

'Well, gee,' said Marianna impatiently, 'I should think doctors would know enough to test for that, after the people get well.'

'They *do* test for it! But suppose you have somebody who's too poor to have a doctor – or doesn't believe in doctors – or isn't very ill and doesn't call a doctor. It's possible to have typhoid and not be very ill. Then nobody knows about it.'

'Couldn't the kid have given it to her grandmother?'

'Certainly. But there's no way of knowing. And where did *she* get it?'

'Can't the patients remember what they were doing the day they got it?'

'They don't know what day it was, Marianna! Typhoid takes from one to three weeks to show symptoms, according to the person's resistance.'

'Who had it first?'

'He didn't say – and it doesn't matter. It doesn't prove which one gave it to the other – if at all. They might have got it on the same day from the one source, whatever it is. Not another soul in the family has had typhoid, and none of them show any signs of it now. Bill's nearly out of his mind trying to trace the thing.'

'Well, if there isn't any more around, why worry?'

'*Goodness*, Marianna –'

Kit glanced at the clock and stood up. 'Come on, old thing! Have typhoid later. You ought to be packing. I'll help if you like. I'll even pop down and do your eggs.'

Sue's jaw dropped conspicuously. 'Did you just say what I thought you said?'

Kit paused in the doorway. 'Why, no, dear,' she said earnestly. 'I never opened my mouth.' She was gone before Sue could think of a sufficiently biting reply to this. Marianna followed a moment later.

Left alone, Sue dawdled over her dressing. She knew that she ought to hurry, that there was a great deal yet to be done, but every garment she put on seemed to bring her nearer to the moment of departure, to the final break with her old life and all that it had meant to her – friends, work, growing up. Kit and Marianna would be with her again – in time – but everything would be different then. She'd be married. Once she had made the break – was on the train, even, this afternoon – she'd begin looking forward instead of back – she always did – but just now, at the last minute, it was hard to let go.

'I'm exactly like Johnny Mackin,' she thought. Johnny had been one of Sue's patients when she was in training. He was eleven years old, but he fought and shrieked when his mother left him the first day. The nurses had had to hold him until the ward door closed behind her. Johnny had given a final bellow, and then, with a gulp of resignation, had turned to the nurses. 'Hello,' he had said with a tearful grin.

She smiled, remembering; then, moving more briskly, pulled on her suit skirt and ran downstairs, fastening it up as she went.

After breakfast Sue and Kit packed. Marianna waited on them both, and by noon the chaos in Sue's room had been reduced to a few odds and ends. There was a hurried lunch, eaten in the kitchen and standing up, and if the general tone of gaiety had a forced quality at times the girls carefully ignored it. They spoke chiefly of the day when Kit and Marianna would come to the hospital at Winslow.

'If we could only come now,' Kit said. 'But a little more Henry Street won't do me any harm.'

'There's me, too,' Marianna put in. 'I gotta finish night high school before I can be a nurse.'

'I know,' said Sue brightly. 'It won't be long. And once you're there fifty miles is no distance at all.'

They assured each other of this a great many times. It was

all going to be marvellous. Sue gesticulated as she talked, her ring sparkling with every movement of her slim hands. Marianna's eyes followed the twinkling points of fire, but she said no more about warnings or bad luck.

Kit telephoned at last for Sue's taxi. There was flurry and tramping, a great upheaval of luggage, and a final crowding into the dim, tobacco-smelling car. Except for one bad moment when Sue looked back through the taxi window at the little house, the next to the last step of her break with her old life was accomplished before she realized it. There remained only the minutes in the station.

This was harder to carry off well, for there was a long wait on the platform, with Sue leaning out of the window looking at the girls' upturned faces, and trying to pretend that nothing was happening. How many times Kit had seen her off on trains! It had been Kit and Connie for a long while. Now it was Kit and Marianna. But this time was different. Connie must have felt like this, too.

The smoky, clamouring station faded for a brief instant as Sue recalled an evening two years ago, when all the old crowd had been gathered in the living-room of the Nurses' Home, at the hospital. Everyone was bursting with plans for new jobs, and Kit was elaborating on the adventures she and Sue would have at Henry Street. Connie, who was going to be married – to a man with whom she was deeply in love – had said nothing at all, looking from one to the other with oddly bright eyes. Sue understood that look, now.

'Well,' Kit was saying lightly, 'we'll be seeing you at the wedding.'

Sue swallowed – and laughed. 'You will unless Bill gets cold feet and deserts me at the altar.' She turned to the big-eyed Marianna. '*You* let me know what train you're coming on, Marianna, and get Kit on it! She always misses trains.'

'Sure,' said Marianna sturdily. 'I'll have her there.'

Somehow the moments passed, and then, abruptly, the train began to move. The girls' good-byes were lost in the gathering roar. They stood waving, growing smaller and smaller until they were two dots at the small far end of the platform.

Sue pulled her head in at last – to find the ticket-collector beside her, and was startled to hear her own voice saying to him rather weakly:

'Oh, hello!'

3

Storm brewing

THAT was the nice thing about home – nothing changed. Everything was just as it had always been, ever since Sue could remember. In the kitchen, Mary, the hired girl, was singing with more volume than tune while she washed the first instalment of luncheon dishes. The faint clear chime of a bell buoy in the harbour accompanied her. Beyond the snowy reach of the Bartons' lawn, where the river tide raced between icy banks, gulls wheeled and screamed under a heavy sky. Mary's voice soared upwards. 'Roo-o-ock of A-a-aa-ages, cleft for me-ee –'

'I wish,' said Mrs. Barton mildly, 'that she'd learn something else.' She glanced towards the windows. 'Oh, dear,' she added, 'I'm afraid we're going to have a bad storm. I don't like the sky when it's slaty like that.'

Luncheon was almost over and Sue, who had talked until late the night before, and steadily all the morning, was at last talked out. She leaned back in her chair, relaxed and content, pleasantly aware of the room and its occupants. It was odd, she reflected, how differently you saw things as you grew older – the dining-room, for instance. She had never really looked at it before, as a whole, yet all these years it had been a lovely room, graciously proportioned, and furnished with Chippendale and Sheraton that would have done credit to any museum.

Sue smiled, remembering how she and Ted had teased their mother about her passion for antiques, complaining bitterly of little knobs that came off in careless young hands, of scroll-work which Sue had dusted so many times in a fury of dislike. Now, suddenly, it was beautiful. 'Mother's really an artist in her way,' Sue thought. 'I never realized –'

She glanced from one to the other of her parents, her eyes tender and indulgent. Dr. Barton was finishing his coffee, staring absently out of the window at the solid mass of grey clouds. His hair was all white now, and thinning, and there were lines round his eyes. 'Oh no!' Sue thought, 'Daddy darling – you mustn't get old!' But he was, and there was nothing she could do about it.

Mrs. Barton had changed very little. Her hair had been white for so long that one did not associate it with advancing years. She had always been plump, always been dignified, always had those round young eyes – the eyes of a little girl astonished at finding herself grown up. Sue wondered if it seemed strange to her mother to have two great oafs like Ted and herself around, instead of those sweet babies.

Ted Junior's place at the table was vacant, for he was away at school and would not be home until it was time for Sue's wedding. Mrs. Barton must have been thinking of this, for she turned to Sue.

'Darling,' she began, transferring an infinitesimal breadcrumb from the tablecloth to her plate, 'if you could just decide on the exact date. I'm afraid you don't realize how much there is to be done – all this coming so suddenly. The invitations have to go out – there's your grandmother's wedding dress to –'

'I do realize, Mummy – really I do. But you see it depends on when Bill can get someone to take his practice while he's gone. He'll be –'

The telephone in the hall rang sharply.

'That's Bill!' said Sue with certainty. Her eyes were bright as she vanished into the hall.

Dr. Barton twinkled at his wife and she smiled in response.

Outside in the hall Sue picked up the receiver and sat down, tense, on the edge of a chair. 'Hello?'

There was no answer for a moment. Then the operator said briskly, 'Springdale calling Miss Sue Barton.'

'Speaking!' Sue relaxed and leaned back, crossing one slim leg over the other. A dimple appeared at the corner of her mouth.

'Here's your call,' said the operator. 'Go ahead.'

'Hello?' said Sue again, and Bill's voice replied, close against her ear in the dimness of the hall. It was to be a long while before Sue was to hear gaiety in his voice again.

'Hello, darling!'

'Good afternoon, Dr. Barry. Is that any way to address your future Visiting Nurse?'

'It depends on the nurse.' The warmth in his tone reached out to her across the miles. 'Some women are like that, you know. They expect it.'

'Oh, *do* they? That's just dandy!'

'Yes, isn't it? Makes everything so simple.'

'It would, of course – and so nice for you.'

'Ouch!' said Bill tenderly. 'Now I know it's you talking. Could you bear to see me?'

'I'll try. When were you thinking of coming?'

'Saturday afternoon – if the icy roads don't hold me up.'

The dimple vanished. 'Oh, Bill! *Please* be careful!'

The sudden intake of Bill's breath was distinctly audible. 'Sue, darling – are you worrying about – me?'

A composite picture of every accident case Sue had ever seen rose before her. 'Certainly not!' she faltered. 'I – I'd get fun – out of – seeing you sandwiched between an overturned car and the road. It's –'

'Oh, darling! I'm so sorry! I didn't think. I only meant to explain why I might be late. It's perfectly all right – really.' Then, as there was no reply, he added, 'I promise to turn up without a scratch.'

'Please do,' said Sue at last. 'It would be sort of more fun if you got here without broken bones. Because now I come to think of it – I've had a vague notion of getting married to you – just an impulse, of course.'

'Like the idea?'

'It seemed all right at the time.'

'Does it still?'

'What do you think?'

'Want me to tell you – right now – in front of the operator?'

'Never mind,' said Sue hastily. She considered for an instant. Then, 'Bill, is everything all right up there?'

'Why, yes. There've been a few small annoying things – but nothing important except the typhoids.'

'You still haven't traced the infection?'

'Not yet.'

'And no more cases?'

'No.'

'It's the oddest thing!'

'You're telling me!' said Bill with feeling.

'All right, then – see you Saturday.'

'Hey! You're not going?'

'Of course I'm going! This must be costing you millions!'

Bill groaned. 'I might have known it. You're going to turn out to be one of these practical females – a domineering woman, no doubt. I can just see you ten years from now – hard-eyed, thin-lipped, determined –'

'Well, naturally.' The dimple had returned. 'After ten years of being married to you! And I might as well start practising now. Good-bye, Dr. Barry – until Saturday.'

Sue hung up quickly and rose, slim, laughing, vibrant with happiness. She was still flushed when she returned to the dining-room to encounter her mother's bewildered eyes and her father's broad smile.

'Your mother,' Dr. Barton said, 'finds your style of conversation with your future husband a little startling.'

'Oh, I wouldn't say that,' Mrs. Barton put in hastily. 'But it *is* a little different from my young days. I can't imagine *what* your father would have thought if I'd talked to him like that. But I suppose it's the fashion now to be flippant.'

'How did you talk to him, Mummy?' said Sue, sliding into her chair without pulling it any farther out – exactly as she had done as a child. 'Don't tell me you called Daddy "Mister" up to your very wedding day.'

'Well – no – but I hope I was always modest and retiring.'

'Goodness! Daddy, how did you ever bring her to the point of saying she'd marry you?'

'Mm,' said Dr. Barton reminiscently. 'Well, you see she told me that she considered it very improper for a young man to kiss a girl unless they were engaged. So, of course, after that buggy ride – you remember that buggy ride, Mama?'

'Really, Ted –' Mrs. Barton began.

'Mummy!' Sue cried, enchanted. 'You're blushing! Look at her, Daddy! What *happened*?'

Dr. Barton chuckled. 'Oh – well, it seemed to me, thinking about that buggy ride later, that in view of the shock to your mother's sense of propriety, the least I could do would be to ask her at once to become engaged to me.'

'Your father is exaggerating as usual,' Mrs. Barton said crisply. 'I'm sure I behaved no differently from any other nice girl.'

'That's what I've always surmised,' Dr. Barton said heartily.

In the laughter that followed Sue glanced curiously at her parents. She had never thought of them in relation to anything but herself, and the revelation of them as the young engaged couple of long ago was oddly surprising. They were still in love, too, after all these years. 'Oh, I hope Bill and I will be like that,' she thought.

The telephone rang again, and the call, this time, was for Dr. Barton. He returned from it to stand for a moment in the doorway.

'The Leighton baby is on the way,' he said briefly. 'It'll be an all-night session.' His shoulders sagged a little, resuming their burden of effort, and Sue remembered that the Leightons lived far out in the country.

Mrs. Barton rose at once. 'Then you'll want your heavy overcoat, dear,' she said capably. 'Have you got chains on the car? I'm afraid this storm is going to be bad.' She bustled out of the room, and Dr. Barton followed her with the docility of a child.

Sue pushed back her chair and crossed to the window to

stare out at the slaty sky. A few thin flakes were already wavering past the window and from far out in the harbour's mouth she heard the long moan of the fog-horn. The front door closed with a jar and a moment later Sue heard her mother's step.

'Mummy,' she said without turning, 'Bill's going to drive down!'

'Well, dear,' Mrs. Barton said quietly, 'this is only Thursday, and from what you said over the telephone I gathered that he wasn't coming until Saturday. The storm will surely be over by then.'

'Yes, but if it's a bad storm the roads will still be awful, and – and I suppose he's out in it somewhere, now.'

'So is your father.'

There was a little silence. Then Sue turned slowly to her mother. 'I suppose,' she said, 'that you've felt like this with every storm Daddy's been out in. I never realized before.'

'Yes,' Mrs. Barton said simply, 'I have. But it's worth it.'

Sue caught her lower lip in her teeth. Then she said softly, 'Thank you, Mummy. I'm glad you said that. I thought it *would* be worth it, but when you're just beginning you can't be sure.'

They looked at one another, for the first time not as mother and daughter, but as woman to woman – a long look of understanding and mutual support.

'Don't worry any more, dear,' Mrs. Barton said at last. 'He can always come on the train, and of course he will if the roads are blocked.' She raised herself on tiptoe to kiss Sue and went away.

She turned back to the window. The flakes were a white smother now. She could barely see the river. And the wind was beginning to rise, swirling the snow across the deserted lawn. Sue watched it, her forehead pressed against the icy window-pane, and presently, quite unaware of what she was doing, she began to twist her ring round and round on her finger.

4

The storm breaks

THE snow continued all night, driven by a trumpeting wind.
It was a wild storm, and it was to set in motion events – small
only in their beginnings – which were to affect Sue's life after
the storm itself had been forgotten. Meanwhile the dark
shadow of the immediate future, unaffected by the weather,
was creeping upon Sue, minute by minute. She slept peacefully,
not knowing.

Towards dawn Dr. Barton came home from the Leightons'
and Sue, waking briefly into hissing darkness, heard her
mother padding down the stairs, and then, presently, a murmur
of voices in the kitchen – punctuated as always by the thin
distant clang of the bell buoy.

Sue turned over, drowsily aware of the comfortable warmth
that was bed, and slept again. When she woke it was broad
daylight. The wind had blown itself out, and the falling snow
was only a scattering of great white feathers, drifting aimlessly
on the still air. Drifts stood high round the house, banking the
windows, and the downstairs rooms lay in a strange twilight.
Out of doors everything familiar had vanished. There was only
white snow, and a silver sky.

Sue meant to go ski-ing, but her skis were in the attic; they
would have to be waxed – and somehow the morning was gone
before she realized the fact. At noon the sky came suddenly
down. It came endlessly, falling straight, and silent except for a
little pelting whisper, an interminable sigh. There was no
breath of wind – only that white curtain piling downwards
forever on sheeted roofs and cotton trees.

It fell all the afternoon and all the evening. It was still falling when the family went upstairs to bed at eleven o'clock.

Sue, who had been drowsy all day, was now wide awake and,

36

after trying for a time to read herself to sleep, at last got up, and pulling on warm dressing-gown and slippers went down to the kitchen for a glass of hot milk – the nurse's standard remedy for sleeplessness. A little later, carrying the steaming glass, she wandered into the living-room, and finding the fire still alive, threw on a fresh log and sat down in her father's arm-chair to toast her feet on the hearth. She didn't bother to put on a light. The fire gave light enough, and as the new log caught, the shadows started up from the corners to dance over furniture and walls. Sparks snapped, and a faint smoky scent of autumn woods crept out of the fireplace. Outside, the snow whispered against the windows, and far away the bell buoy chimed.

She was comfortable and growing sleepy. She thought of the girls. Marianna, at this moment, was probably asleep in Sue's bed. Or perhaps she and Kit hadn't gone up yet. And Connie – little dark-haired Connie, bubbling with laughter. She was in Boston, in the new house Phil had bought. Sue had never seen it and now, drowsily, she tried to imagine it from the descriptions in Connie's letters.

The sound outside, when it came, was felt rather than heard – a faint vibration of the ground, a kind of soundless beat muffled by snow.

The drowsiness fled from Sue's eyes. She sat upright in the grip of a sudden, unreasonable apprehension. She knew that it was unreasonable. Some motorist was undoubtedly stuck in the snow and coming to use the telephone; or somebody wanted Dr. Barton. That was all, surely.

Sue listened, every muscle tense. The sound had reached the porch now, and she waited for the knocker to strike. There was only an unaccountable silence. Sue's fingers tightened round the hot glass.

Then she heard a voice, low and urgent, close to the front door.

'Sue!'

Sue put down the glass and sprang to her feet. The front

door stuck, but she got it loose at last and flung it open into a
swirl of snowflakes and cold air. A tall, shadowy figure stepped
out of the gloom and caught her in its arms.

'*Bill!*' she gasped against a wet camel's-hair shoulder.
'*What –*'

Lips cold from the wind, the roughness of an unexpected
moustache, were hard against her mouth. '*Oh, my dearest!*'
she heard. '*My sweet!*' The whispered words had a quality of
strange, fierce protectiveness, and the arms round her were,
suddenly, iron walls.

'What *is* it?' she asked, a little dazed.

'Come inside, darling. You'll catch your death out here.'

In the dimness of the hall Bill took off his coat and hat,
shook the snow from them, and hung them on the rack. Sue
stared at him, speechless – questioning. Even in that light she
could see that his face was white and drawn, that there were
dark circles under his eyes – but the firm lines of his mouth
under the new moustache were unaltered, steady, tender. He
turned from the coat-rack to slip an arm round Sue and draw
her into the living-room, to the warmth of the fire. Its light
played over him as he faced her, outlining against the wall
behind him his narrow hips, breadth of shoulder, and fine dark
head. His eyes, meeting hers, were heavy with fatigue – and
something else.

'What *is* it, Bill? *Please* tell me!'

'Darling,' Bill began, 'I –' He paused and then went on
more steadily. 'Sue – my – father is dead.'

'*Oh, Bill dear!*' Sue was motionless with horror. He had
loved his father so much.

'The – cable – came this noon,' he said. 'Eliot sent it. There
was a car accident. I didn't want to telephone you. I had to
see you.'

Sue's hands went out to him and he drew her close.

'Darling,' he said gently, before she could speak, 'I – I'm
afraid this is going to be very bad for – us.' His arms were steel
bands, holding her.

She looked up at him, scarcely realizing his last remark. She was trying to find words that would help him, and there were no words.

He stared over her head into the shadows. 'It – it means,' he went on, 'that we can't be married – not for a long time, anyway. I shall have to take care of my brother.'

There was an instant of stunned silence. Then Sue recovered herself and stirred in his arms, her fingers tightening on his. There were words for this. Here was something she could do.

'Don't worry about us,' she said. 'We'll be all right. Of course you have to take care of your brother!'

'You don't understand, dear. It'll be a long time. I've no right to ask you to wait –'

'Don't be silly!' said Sue sharply. 'Of course I'll wait. You waited for me long enough. I'm in this, too. You can't just set me outside and take it all yourself.'

'But –'

'*No!*'

'Oh, Sue!'

They clung together for a moment, then Sue whispered into his tie, 'That's settled then.'

Bill released her. 'You always come through, don't you?' he said tenderly.

But Sue was looking at the drawn lines round his mouth. 'Goodness,' she exclaimed, 'what a fool I am! You're exhausted! I – the drive down must have been – sit down, Bill! I'm going to make you some coffee.'

When she returned with a laden tray he was sitting in her father's arm-chair. His bigness filled it, and his long legs were stretched out on the hearth. He turned his head to look at her as she came in and she was relieved to see that his lean cheeks were less taut, his mouth under the dark line of moustache definitely relaxed.

The colour crept into his face as he ate the sandwiches she had made and drank the steaming hot coffee. Sue drew up a chair beside his and waited. When he had finished she said,

'Do you feel like talking things over, Bill, or would you rather not, for a while?'

'I'd rather, darling. That's what I came for.' He reached out for her hand, and clasped it in both of his as he talked. 'You see, Dad –' The words stopped him for a second and he went on with an effort. 'Dad never saved any money. He didn't pay any attention to it. There'll be hardly enough to get Eliot back from abroad.'

'Yes, dear, I understand. Go on.'

'Eliot's only eighteen and he's a cripple. He has to have a male nurse. He must go on with his electrical and radium treatments. And he must go through university. With an education he'll be able to earn a living.'

'And you can swing all that if we don't get married?'

'I can if I give up the house, and Mrs. Cooney, and take two small rooms in the village. And in a couple of years Eliot ought to be able to get a really decent scholarship. Then I'll have only his medical bills – and we can be married.'

'*In a couple of years!* Oh, Bill – I thought you meant five or ten!'

'Good Lord!' said Bill, shocked. 'I *am* sorry! I've been driving so long behind those rotten snow-ploughs – telling you all about it in my mind – that I forgot you wouldn't know that.' He caught her hand against his lips in apology.

Sue swallowed the lump in her throat. All those long hours alone, creeping behind the ploughs, facing his father's death and their shattered hopes!

'It's all right,' she said gently. 'And two years isn't very long.' She paused, thinking. 'Bill,' she said suddenly, 'I'm coming to Springdale, and I'm going to be your assistant – just as we'd planned. I don't see why we have to be separated for two years.'

He stared at her blankly.

'But there's no one to pay you, Sue. It was different when we were to have been married – when you would have shared my income –'

'I'll find somebody to pay me! There's always some way –'

'Wait a minute!' Bill said. 'God knows I'd give my eyes to have you there – but you couldn't earn a living in Springdale as a nurse – unless you got a job with the State Visiting Nurse Association – and they've a waiting list of nurses –'

'I don't want a job with the State Visiting Nurse Association! I could be transferred anywhere, at any time. The first thing I knew I'd be at the other end of the state, working for old Dr. Diddlepop, Health Officer in Scrabble-among-the-Sticks. I'm working with *you*!'

'But, darling, Springdale is just a village, and while it's not poor, neither is it rich. There just isn't anybody to pay the salary of an independent Visiting Nurse. Because even if the townspeople approved of the idea they wouldn't vote for any-thing that would increase their taxes by one penny – not just now, anyway.'

The obstinacy of Sue's chin was suddenly very apparent.

'How do you know,' she demanded, 'that there isn't some nice rich philanthropist who comes there in the summer and would love to give the town a Visiting Nurse – if the idea were brought to his attention?'

'The only rich people,' Bill said patiently, 'who come there in the summer hardly know the town exists – and care less. Besides, they'd say – and quite reasonably, too – that if a Visiting Nurse is necessary, why shouldn't the state provide her?'

'You do need a Visiting Nurse, don't you?'

'Very badly. In fact, at the present time there is one Visiting Nurse to every three thousand population.'

'Mercy! Then why *hasn't* the state provided one?'

'Lack of funds. They do the best they can, and every town has either a school nurse *or* a Visiting Nurse – but there aren't enough of both to go round – and the ones they've got have so much territory to cover that they can only make about one visit a month in any one town.'

'Well,' said Sue, 'there's your answer to any rich man.'

Bill shook his head. 'I'm afraid it won't work, dear. It may seem easy from the outside, but actually you'd have to create both job and funds –'

'I know. That's just what Lillian Wald did.'

'But that was in New York – where there's a lot of money.'

'It's no use arguing, Bill. I'm coming.' Her voice carried such conviction that in spite of all reasoning Bill was impressed.

'You – you darling – sap!' he said, struggling against the contagion of hope. 'If I thought for a minute it could happen – *oh, Sue!*'

'It's going to happen – and that's that!' Sue had been watching his face, and as the fire flared up suddenly her eyes became sharply attentive. 'Bill,' she said, 'is that a bruise under your eye?'

He put up his hand. 'Oh – that? Does it still show? Somebody was heaving stones round in the dark the other night; they seemed to have missed what they were aiming for, and got me instead. It's nothing.'

Sue rose abruptly and came to sit on the arm of his chair. Her fingers were gentle, touching the bruise. *Had* the stone missed its aim? She wondered. 'The sooner I get to Springdale, the better,' she thought.

Bill rested his head against her shoulder and closed his eyes. The lids were blue with fatigue and even as Sue looked down at him, pitying, he was asleep. She changed her position slightly, so that he might rest more comfortably against her, and sat looking at the sparkle of her ring in the firelight. Her lips trembled only once – and then became a firm line.

She hadn't moved, an hour later, when Mrs. Barton, wakened by some habitual, maternal misgiving, saw the light still on in Sue's bedroom and, finding the room empty, came softly downstairs.

5

Springdale

BILL left the next afternoon to make immediate arrangements for closing his house. He looked better after a long sleep, and Sue, feeling that activity and attention to practical details would be the best thing for him, had not urged him to stay. Her father and mother, shocked and deeply sympathetic, were entirely in accord with this point of view, and before he went it was settled that Sue was to follow on Monday – Mrs. Barton to come with her, both as chaperon and as moral support while Sue tried to create a job out of nothing.

Neither Dr. nor Mrs. Barton believed it could be done, but there seemed no reason why Sue shouldn't try. Sue, herself, refused to consider the possibility of failure. 'I'll get that job,' she said, 'if I have to disguise myself as an elderly gentleman who wants to give the town a million dollars!'

How she was to proceed she hadn't the faintest idea. 'I'll just have to wait until I get there,' she told her mother, 'and hope for the best.'

Under ordinary circumstances Sue would have found the drive to Springdale exciting. She would have watched for the first glimpse of the White Mountains, piled in dazzling white against an ice-blue sky. She would have cried out when the car rounded a bend and she saw Mount Washington, its summit hidden in frost clouds, and all the lower peaks of the Presidential Range sweeping away into the distance. Now she scarcely saw them, and even missed a dog team close at hand, streaming across an open field in a smoke of powdered snow.

Her hands gripped the wheel of Mrs. Barton's little coupé with unconscious tensity and she leaned forward, cheeks flushed and eyes serious, scarcely aware of the road and totally unaware of the picture she made – red-gold curls shining under the tiny

astrakhan hat which she wore at a charming and futile angle
on the side of her head. Mrs. Barton glanced at her from time
to time, but said nothing, realizing that Sue was deep in her
problem, and that no practical help could be given her without a knowledge of Springdale – of which Mrs. Barton had
none.

Once, as the drive was nearing its end, Mrs. Barton remarked,
'Sue, I should think this Mrs. Cooney would be a good person
to help you. She seems to be a native of the town.'

'That's true,' said Sue. 'I'll see how she turns out. I certainly
ought to know a little about the people – or I'll go springing
wisecracks on Mr. Whoozit, who thinks women should be seen
and not heard – or go deadly serious with Mr. Whatnot, who
likes clinging women, full of innocent prattle.'

The little car reached Springdale by mid-afternoon, over a
road that tilted downwards in hairpin turns to the floor of a
narrow valley rimmed by mountains. Sue's pulse quickened
as she looked down.

'So that's Springdale,' she said lightly to her mother.

'Yes, dear. Pretty, isn't it?'

A river wandered through the valley – the overflow from
a lake whose waters curved out of sight in the distance – and
the town had been built along both banks, its trim white
houses joined to their barns and set well apart from each other
down the entire length of the valley. Small stone bridges
spanned the river at intervals, and the bare branches of willows
were a fragile lacework above the ice. A town hall, a church,
and a large new school were the only public buildings. Sue was
astonished at the size of the school until she glanced up along
the shoulders of the mountains and saw the farms and, in
smaller valleys, tiny villages. Sue counted five of these and
guessed that there were others hidden in the folds of the hills.
No wonder Bill complained that there was work enough for
half a dozen doctors! There must also be work for that many
nurses – and there was only a school nurse making monthly
visits!

'Goodness!' Sue thought. 'If the town has any sense it will clasp me to its bosom with yells of delight.'

The car rolled into the main street, tyres crackling on hard-packed snow, and stopped at a filling station. The attendant, a lean overalled youth, approached leisurely, and Sue leaned out of the window to inquire about inns.

'Bald Trail Inn's open,' he said, looking at Sue with frank appreciation. 'But it's away up – off there. Bowker's is nearer. It's at t'other end of the town. There's a sign out.'

'Thank you. And could you tell me where Dr. Barry lives?'

The boy pointed to a white colonial house on a jutting cliff high above the village. 'That's hisn – but he's a movin' out.'

'Thank you,' said Sue again, and was releasing her brake when he volunteered suddenly, 'Th' doc ain't there now. He got a call about an hour ago, to go over to Duck Hill. Wun't be back for some while, I guess.'

'Will there be anybody at the house?'

'Ayuh – shouldn't wonder if th' housekeeper was.'

The car moved away, and Sue grinned at Mrs. Barton.

'Well!' she said. 'If you want to know anybody's business round here just ask anybody else.'

'Of course, dear. It's a country village.'

'It certainly is, but it's lovely. Golly! Did you ever see so much snow?'

The car was creeping along white canyons cut through drifts in the main street. Men were still at work, shovelling blocks of snow into waiting trucks, and as the car neared one of these Mrs. Barton exclaimed suddenly, *'Look out, dear!'*

The warning came too late. The front wheel of the car came down on the blade of a shovel which someone had dropped in the snow and the handle flew upwards, striking one of the men across the knuckles. He gave a yelp of pain and swore.

Sue stopped the car and got out.

'Oh, I'm so sorry!' she cried. 'Are you badly hurt?'

The man looked at her and rubbed his hand. 'I ain't real contented,' he said.

Sue almost grinned in spite of her distress. She had been away from New Hampshire so long that she had forgotten the native fondness for understatement.

'May I look at your hand?' she asked. 'I'm a nurse. Perhaps I could do something.'

He held out his hand obediently, looking down at her gravely from his lean height.

The hand was not seriously injured. The knuckles were badly bruised and beginning to swell, but there was no evidence of broken bones. The men round the truck leaned on their shovels, watching while Sue plastered snow on the bruise.

'The cold will keep the swelling down,' she said. 'It's going to be all right – but – I – I'm *awfully* sorry!'

The man's eyes twinkled in his narrow New England face. He had rather nice eyes, Sue noticed.

'No call to git upset,' he said. 'Shouldn't wonder 'f I'd live.'

It was the speech of Sue's childhood and it was pleasant in her ears. Without thinking she replied in kind.

'Seems as though you might,' she said. 'But it's no thanks to me – stramming around like a three-wave sea!'

One of the men watching spoke suddenly. 'Thought ye was city folks,' he said. 'Come frum down-state, don't ye?'

Sue turned to him, nodding. Then, to her uncomfortable victim, 'If you'll give me your name – and if your hand is bad, please let me know – I'll be at Bowker's Inn.'

'Name's Ira Prouty. And don't ye worry a mite about the hand. Likely th' shock'll cure it.'

'Shock?'

'Shouldn't wonder – havin' anybody in a car stop to see what they done.'

Sue had made a friend, and she returned to the car pleasantly aware of the fact. Later she was to wonder at the strange chance which brought her to that particular group of men at that exact moment, and to realize that, had the minor accident with the shovel occurred even half an hour before, or half an hour afterwards, Bill's career in Springdale would, within a year, have come to an end. But at the moment, since Ira Prouty was more uncomfortable than injured, she dismissed the matter as of no great importance.

Bowker's Inn was small, neat, and comfortable. Sue and Mrs. Barton engaged a room, and then, leaving their bags, drove the skidding little car up the road to Bill's house on the bluff.

'I'll wait in the car until you find out if anyone's at home,' Mrs. Barton said, as Sue got out.

'All right, Mummy.'

Sue, up to this point, had managed to keep her thoughts away from her postponed wedding. What was done was done, and there was no use in moaning about it. Besides, it was all much worse for Bill than for her, and in either case readjustment to the new state of affairs was the important thing. But now, with Bill's house before her – the house which would have been *theirs* – she had a sudden pang of realization.

It was a lovely old place, standing well back from the road among its elms – a solidly built house, substantial and dignified, a house of which she could have been proud. It was here that she would have come as a bride, Bill gay beside her. It was here that they would have built their life together. Now someone else would live in their house, and she and Bill – Sue fought back the tears which blinded her so that she could scarcely see the path to the front door.

'You little fool!' she told herself. 'You *would* have to start dripping at the most inopportune moment.' She stood motionless for an instant, trying to regain her self-command, falling back desperately on her sense of humour. 'Anybody'd think,' she said aloud fiercely, 'that it was an old-fashioned film! Beautiful heroine staggers up path to lost home bellowing like anything and slipping on her frozen tears!'

She grinned mistily and sounded the knocker on the front door.

There were answering footsteps, unhurried but firm, and the door was opened by a woman of perhaps fifty, with a serene face and shrewd grey eyes, friendly and twinkling.

'Mrs. Cooney?' said Sue, liking her instantly.

'I be. And you're Miss Barton, I guess. I was expectin' of you.' The hand extended to Sue was plump but shapely, with capable fingers. 'Didn't your mother come?'

'She's in the car.'

'Land, child! It's real sharp out – she'll freeze a settin' there!'

The firm steps went down the path to the car. 'I'm real glad to meet you,' Sue heard. 'Come right along in. I got coffee waitin'. Mind the ice, now. 'Tain't no weather underfoot.'

Mrs. Barton was bundled out of the car and into the house, and Sue began to feel more cheerful. Mummy had been right. Here was the person to come to for advice. 'And I'll come,' she thought, 'the first minute politeness will let me!'

Mrs. Cooney served them coffee in the kitchen – the only room in the house not in a state of confusion and partial dismantlement. It was a pleasant room, crowded with homely, hard-worn things which, Sue guessed, had originally belonged to Mrs. Cooney. Bill might just possibly have chosen the red-and-white checked tablecloth, but he was not likely to have brought home the violently pink-and-green calendar on the wall, or the carved wooden clock, or the ancient rocker by the stove. Even the coffee cups – hand-painted and gaudy – must have been Mrs. Cooney's.

Sue longed to ask if there had been any more of the peculiar demonstrations against Bill, but she didn't want to worry her mother. It would be better to wait until she could talk with Mrs. Cooney alone.

Mrs. Cooney moved serenely between stove and table, replenishing cups, slicing bread with swift, sure movements, putting another stick of wood in the stove, lighting the lights.

'It gets dark dretful early up here,' she said. 'The mountains is real sightly, but they cut off a good deal of sun this time of year.'

Sue put down her cup.

'Mrs. Cooney,' she began, 'I'd like to ask your advice. Mother said you'd be the one to help me.'

'Land! I dunno's I'd say that, but I'm right up and comin'
when 't comes to ladlin' out advice. I can do that faster 'n a
horse can trot.'

'That's just what I want,' said Sue heartily, and plunged into
an account of her plans – her face bright with enthusiasm.
Mrs. Cooney drew up a chair and sat listening, plump elbows
on the red-and-white checked tablecloth. From time to time
her eyes encountered Mrs. Barton's across the table and the two
women exchanged glances, Mrs. Barton's dubious and questioning, Mrs. Cooney's comfortingly quiet.

Sue finished with a rush, her head with its tumbled curls
flung back, and her shoulders determinedly squared. She looked
poised for flight in any direction.

Mrs. Cooney took in the set of Sue's round chin and the
slender young shoulders. She also took in Sue's nervous fiddling
with the coffee spoon, and the slim foot twisting and untwisting
on the rung of the chair.

'Sakes, child!' Mrs. Cooney said. 'Ye remind me of one of
them little sparrer hawks. Ye got courage, I'll say that for ye.
And I wun't say it ain't no use. I've always held that if ye go
after a thing long enough – and hard enough – ye'll get it,
especially when it's folks you're dealin' with. They can hold
out about so long, and then it's too much trouble, and all of a
suddent they let go all holt – and there ye be.'

Sue relaxed. 'Oh, I hoped you'd look at it that way! Bill was
so gloomy about my chances that I –'

'Shucks! A man in love always thinks his girl couldn't git
up off a chair without she'd break. Not that it ain't goin' to be
hard sleddin' – he's right about that. I wouldn't say your chances
was fightin' to git to ye, but there's two wags to a dog's tail –
one forrard and one back. When things git about's fur as
they can one way they're bound to git a goin' in the other.'

Mrs. Barton had been listening anxiously, her absurdly young
eyes going from Mrs. Cooney to Sue. Now she spoke.

'Don't you think Sue had better give up the whole idea? I
hadn't quite realized –'

'Land, no! 'Twun't do no harm to try. And seems like the child'll fly to pieces if she don't do sumpthin'.'

Sue flashed a quick, grateful look at Mrs. Cooney. 'Who should I see?' she asked.

'One of the selectmen – Lot Phinney, I sh'd say. He's got good sense, and if the town can't back ye mebbe he could think of sumpthin'. We need a Visitin' Nurse bad enough, the good Lord knows.'

'What's Mr. Phinney like? I mean, how do I –'

'How do ye act? Just act natural. And don't git the wrong idea about him. He huff-wuffs a good deal, but it don't mean a thing. He's real good-hearted, Lot is, for all he acts like he had the green-apple colic – and he sets considerable store by the doctor. Tell him the hull thing, same's you told me.'

Sue's spirits were rising higher with every minute. Mrs. Cooney's faith in the efficacy of determination was contagious. Sue was beginning to feel that she could do anything, and her courage was further strengthened, on Bill's return, by his delight at seeing her actually in Springdale.

After dinner, while Mrs. Cooney washed the dishes and Mrs. Barton wiped them, Sue and Bill went for a walk. By unspoken agreement they did not mention Bill's father's death; nor did they speak of weddings. They were together and that, just now, was enough.

The stillness of the air was like thin crystal, brittle with cold, and their breaths made a white mist in it. Snow squeaked underfoot, and overhead, through the naked branches of elms, the stars flared green. Beyond the twinkling lights in the valley the mountains were an inky blackness against the slate-blue sky.

Sue's hand was curled in Bill's, in his coat pocket. He had shortened his steps to keep pace with hers, and moved beside her close and comforting. The starlight showed her a lean cheek, the strongly modelled lines of his head, and one broad shoulder. She felt, rather than saw, the warmth in his eyes as he looked down at her.

They talked very little, both of them bruised with their first encounter with tragedy, and not wanting to interrupt with speech the quiet peace of simply being together, with nothing else happening. After a time, as the cold began to bite through their clothing, they turned back, swinging easily over the snow side by side.

Sue slept soundly that night, being young, healthy, and very tired. It was Mrs. Barton who lay awake, uneasy on a strange bed, aware of every sound in the Inn, and worrying about Sue's future. It was dawn when she fell asleep. When she woke the sun was high – and Sue's bed was empty.

Sue's determination was as strong as ever when she stopped her mother's car before the rambling old house which had been pointed out to her as Lot Phinney's.

Mr. Phinney himself opened the door in answer to Sue's pull on the bell. She knew him instantly from Mrs. Cooney's description – 'a leetle mite of a man, kinder stoop-shouldered, grey-haired, wattles like a turkey gobbler, an' reddish-brown eyes that ain't as cross as he thinks they be'.

They were, however, cross enough.

'I ain't buyin' nothing,' he said before Sue could speak.

'Neither am I,' she returned promptly. 'My name is Barton, and I'm –'

'Ye be! The doctor's girl! Whyn't ye say so in the fust place? Heard ye was a redhead. Well! Come in! Come in! No need to stand there like a bump on a log.'

Sue followed him inside to a dusty, cluttered little office, and sat down in the worn cane chair he pushed towards her. Mr. Phinney lowered himself gingerly into a swivel chair and swung round to face her.

'Well – what ye want?'

Sue told him, trying to speak tersely and to the point.

'I think my place is with Bill,' she finished. 'But I'd also like to say that New Hampshire is my own state and I love it. I'd adore working here, even if I'd never heard of Bill. And you need a Visiting Nurse, and I've had about the best training there is.'

Mr. Phinney grunted. 'White hen's chicken, ain't ye?' he said, but the red-brown eyes were not unkind. The swivel chair creaked agonizingly as he swung round to stare out of the window. Sue waited, breathless, and after a moment he turned back to her.

'Ye're honest,' he said. 'I like that in ye. And I like the doctor. There's a lot of poverty back in the hills, as well as plenty of sick folks right here in town. A good nurse would be –' He paused.

Sue straightened in her chair, her eyes suddenly eager.

'Then you think –' she began.

The old man glanced at her unhappily. 'There ain't a soul in town but what would be glad to have ye, but the town can't do it now. In a couple of years – maybe – but not yet. And there ain't a mite of use my bringin' it up, come town meetin'.' He added unexpectedly, 'I'm downright sorry.'

'You – you're very – kind,' Sue faltered. 'I – suppose I shouldn't have – hoped. But I did. Isn't there *any* way?'

The old man folded his hands over his watch chain. Then he said slowly, 'Ye might try Elias Todd. He could do about anything he was of a mind to – if he took the notion.'

'Who's he?'

Mr. Phinney grunted again. 'He's our light in the midst of darkness. Come frum around here 'riginally – born over to Todd's Corners, in fact. Went off to – New York, I think 'twas – and got rich. Millionaire, they tell me. Likes to come back here and strut it in front of us natives. Togs himself out in them baggy pants and raises a whole mess of them little dogs. Cussed little things, they be, 'bout a yard long and an inch high.'

'Oh, you mean dachshunds.'

'Yup. That's as good a name for 'em as any. Guess they kinder make him forget he was born to Todd's Corners.'

'Would he be here now – in winter?'

'Yup. He's got a lot to do with them snow trains comes in for the ski-in'. Owns a hotel over on Bald Trail. Makes a good thing out of it, I guess. Brags a lot, he does, about never gittin' into nothin' that ain't sure-fire. Needs a wife, shouldn't wonder, but I guess he figgers that's too uncertain.'

'What makes you think he might –'

'Likes to strut, I told ye. Might git him that way – grateful natives a cheerin' him to everlastin' glory.' The red-brown eyes twinkled, though Mr. Phinney's face remained grave.

Sue laughed and rose, hopeful again.

'Thank you, Mr. Phinney,' she said, giving him her hand. 'You've helped a lot. When do you think would be a good time to see him?'

'Dunno. He ain't in town right now. Comes and goes. Guess ye'll have to wait around.'

'Thank you. I will. Good-bye, Mr. Phinney.'

Mr. Phinney's weather-beaten face wrinkled into a smile as benevolent as it was unexpected.

'Hope ye skin the eye-teeth right outen him,' he said.

6

'You ain't settled yet'

FOR two weeks Sue waited restlessly for Elias Todd. Meanwhile Bill had a long and rather pathetic letter from his young brother, asking to be allowed to remain where he was and finish out his college year – a suggestion which simplified matters considerably. Bill moved into his rooms in the village, Mrs. Barton went home, and Sue took a room in Mrs. Cooney's grey-shingled little house, which stood high above the town, at the end of the valley.

Mrs. Cooney had urged Sue to stay with her. 'Your mother can't hang around here till doomsday, waitin' on Elias Todd – and ye don't want to be stuck by yourself over to Bowker's. Besides, I'm out of a job now, and I'd be glad to rent a room.'

So Mrs. Barton, feeling that Sue would be in good hands, returned home, and Sue moved in with Mrs. Cooney.

The little house had a breath-taking view of the mountains – range after range of peaks, piled up in frozen silence. Sue's bedroom window faced them – an old-fashioned room with sloping ceiling and sprigged wallpaper – and when she woke in the morning she lay watching the blue shadows creep back up the mountains as the winter sun rose. There were nearly always clouds asleep in the hollows at dawn, and these, too, departed with the sun – in a strangely lifelike manner, for they stretched themselves vastly before they crawled away. Sue could never bear to get up until they had gone.

At noon, having lunch with Mrs. Cooney in the warm sunny little kitchen with its Dutch oven, its painted wood box, and its hand-pump over the iron sink, Sue learned the history of everybody in Springdale. But as she listened her eyes returned, always, to the mountains, sharply white in the sunlight, or dim through falling snow. There was opportunity and to spare, now, to discuss the mysterious attacks on Bill, but they no longer seemed important for the simple reason that they had stopped.

At dusk Sue stood at the window, watching the changing light, until the mountains became black cardboard pasted against a blue-black sky, and it was time for Bill's evening visit.

They were growing very close together now, in a new understanding.

'You're different, did you know it?' Sue remarked one evening. 'You don't get furious with me any more.'

Bill considered, the middle finger of his left hand going to his moustache in an odd little gesture of inquiry. He was beginning to do this habitually, Sue noticed, whenever he was puzzled or reflecting. He was deep in a leather armchair, his long legs stretched out before him, and his suddenly embarrassed glance travelled their entire length to the tips of his toes, before he spoke.

'I was jealous,' he said. 'You're pretty streamlined, you know, and other men saw it – and then you kept putting me off for this career business. I felt about as sure of you as I am of buying a Rolls-Royce at the present time. It's not being sure that makes people jealous.'

'Yes,' Sue agreed. 'I remember the time I thought you were in love with that slinky little –'

'Telephone, doctor,' said Mrs. Cooney from the doorway. 'I guess ye'll have to go. Looroy Crowell's young one has croup – bad.'

'I wish I could go with you,' said Sue wistfully. She had hoped to go with him on his rounds of the countryside, had thought that she could learn a great deal about conditions while she waited, but Mrs. Cooney advised against it.

'Not till ye're official,' she said. 'If you wasn't engaged to him it would be different. As 'tis, folk'll talk. He better just come here to see you.'

That had been the day after Mrs. Barton's return home, and as a result of this edict Sue had little to do, and the time dragged miserably in spite of letters to the girls, long walks in the snow-covered village, and the pleasant evenings with Bill. Sue was accustomed to work, and without it she felt lost. She was accustomed to the lively companionship of Kit and Marianna, too, and one day, missing them more than usual, she had an idea.

'If,' she thought, 'I can manage to get a job here, why shouldn't Marianna come and stay with me? She could go to school here perfectly well. Kit wouldn't care – she'd be glad to get the expense of the house off her hands now I'm not there to share it. Mrs. Cooney would like it, too. She adores having lots of people around.'

Mrs. Cooney was pleased with the suggestion, as Sue had known she would be.

'Of course she can come! For that matter, the two of ye could rent the house, leavin' one room for me – and I could do for ye. But you better hold your horses – ye ain't settled yet. Sure as ye plan to go north you're bound to go south.'

The next day Sue encountered the school nurse, who had parked her car on the main street. Sue, strolling through the quiet street on her daily walk, noticed the Visiting Nurse insignia on the car door – and a pair of skis strapped to the roof. She paused.

'Golly!' she thought. 'That's another thing! I'd have to have a car of my own – and how do I get it? I might as well hope for a gold car studded with diamonds.'

She was still lingering on the sidewalk when the nurse appeared – a pleasant-faced girl, wearing a raccoon coat and the usual black felt hat. A rim of blue skirt, the same colour as Sue's Henry Street uniforms, showed beneath the hairy bottom of the coat.

'Hello,' said Sue.

'Hello.'

They smiled at one another.

'I was looking at your car,' Sue explained. 'I'm a nurse, too, from the Henry Street Settlement in New York, and I –'

'*Henry Street!*' The nurse was openly flustered. 'I'd like so much to talk to you. We – our state organization is patterned on Henry Street as nearly as possible, but I never met a real Henry Street nurse before, and –'

'You can't possibly want to talk to me as much as I want to talk to you. I need advice *so* badly –'

The nurse laughed. 'Come on! Let's sit in my car, out of this wind. Oh – and my name is Mowbray.'

'And I'm Sue Barton.'

As they climbed into the car Sue noticed a pair of snowshoes on the back seat. 'Are you quite sure you're a nurse?' she asked, sitting down. 'You wouldn't, maybe, be an agent in disguise – for a sporting-goods firm?'

'What – *oh!* The snowshoes!'

'And skis.'

Miss Mowbray settled herself behind the wheel. 'They're more or less standard equipment,' she said. 'And in summer I usually carry a canoe paddle on the back seat. More than once I've had to help myself to somebody's boat.'

'Golly! What fun!'

'Well, you never know – but tell me – what's the trouble?'

And so, for the millionth time, it seemed to Sue, she told her story, only to find Miss Mowbray as doubtful as everyone else.

'I don't know,' she said, and poor Sue thought that nobody, *ever*, seemed to know. 'Of course, it goes without saying that a Public Health Nurse is needed here. Our girls have to cover such a fearful lot of territory. But that isn't much help, is it? I can't tell you much about Todd – except that he'll probably try to make passes at you. I don't think it means anything. He's just trying to live up to his picture of himself as something pretty special.'

'That'll be lovely!'

'Wait a second!' Miss Mowbray brightened. 'There *is* one thing! The American Red Cross is wonderful about supplementing nurses' salaries – or providing a car and supplies. You'll have to have a car, naturally, and if you can persuade Elias to put up your salary I'm almost certain the Red Cross would furnish the car and medical supplies. You might mention that to him. It might impress him.'

'He sounds too awful!' Sue wailed. 'I feel as if I'd have to go to see him in a parade, with "Sue Barton, the President's Choice" on all the banners, and a string of Bathing Beauties well up in front.'

'I know. But still – his kind are usually easy to manage, because you know what to expect.'

Sue reflected that there were always exceptions to any rule, and hoped that Mr. Todd would not be one. Nevertheless, she was encouraged by her talk with Miss Mowbray. The possibility of help from the Red Cross was something definite to put forward.

'I can't afford to neglect any possibility,' she thought. 'Because Mr. Todd is certainly my last chance. If *he* doesn't come through I – I'll be so far up in the air that even the birds couldn't find me. Oh, Lord! I do wish he'd come so that I could get it over!'

Mr. Todd, however, remained away, and before Sue's nervous anticipations had time to develop much further they were completely side-tracked by the outbreak of another case of typhoid.

Three days later there were two more.

'I simply can't understand it!' Bill told Sue that night, pacing back and forth in Mrs. Cooney's front room. 'They're all men, this time – not that that signifies anything. They live in different parts of the village – none of them have been near the first two cases – and nobody in their families has ever had typhoid! I've already had all the water and milk in town analysed.' He ran his fingers through his dark hair, ruffling it into wild spears and tufts. 'What's more,' he added, stopping abruptly before the wing chair in which Sue was sitting, 'there's been almost *no* typhoid in New Hampshire – and hasn't been in years.'

'Have you analysed the brooks and springs outside the town?'

'*Of course I have!*' He resumed his pacing. 'At least, the

Board of Health attended to it, after I sent in my report on the first cases – over a month ago.'

Sue leaned on the chair arm, chin in hand, her troubled eyes following Bill's tall figure in its erratic progress over Mrs. Cooney's Brussels carpet.

'You're pretty sure about its being a carrier, aren't you?' she said at last.

Bill turned, jamming one hand violently into his trousers' pocket. '*Of course it's a carrier!*' he almost shouted. 'It can't be anything else! But *who? Where?*'

Sue's eyes met his. She said gently, 'I'm not on the top of Mount Washington – and my hearing is perfectly good.'

Bill reached out and touched a curl on Sue's forehead. 'I'm sorry, sweet. I didn't realize –'

'I know you didn't.' Sue drew her feet closer under her and sat thinking. After a moment Bill lowered himself to the floor beside her chair, folding up like a pocket rule, his arms clasped around his knees, his worried young face turned to Sue.

The fire in the open grate crackled cheerfully, and the wind sang round the corners of the house, stirring the air in the warm room a little, so that the potted ferns near the windows nodded.

'Bill,' said Sue at last, 'tell me about these last cases. I mean, who are they, and what do they do?'

'Everything in summer. In winter they have pretty steady jobs shovelling snow for the town.'

'Shovelling snow? Do they work together?'

'Yes, they do – but it doesn't prove a thing, because there are five men in that particular road gang. Three have come down with typhoid, and the other two have no symptoms at all. I saw every one of them today, and took blood tests. Your friend Ira Prouty is one of the two who have no symptoms.'

'And they can't remember eating or drinking anything given them by a mysterious stranger in a long black cape with his hat brim pulled down over his face?'

'No. They can't remember a thing – not even a strange woman in white haunting Fogg's store, and calling to them to come up and see her and have a spot of milk prepared and personally infected by her.'

'That's true. Carriers are more apt to be women, aren't they?'

'So I was told when I was a little boy in medical school, though there *have* been quite a few men carriers.' He paused, and then remarked suddenly, 'It's not so easy to remember. Let's hear you tell me everything you've eaten or drunk in the last ten days – and exactly where you ate it or drank it!'

'*Heavens!* Yes – I see what you mean. Are they very ill, Bill?'

'Two are – poor devils!'

'Don't you want me to – I mean, couldn't I do a little nursing for you?'

'I'm sending them to Winslow Hospital, darling, thanks just the same. That's another thing. I'll have to go all the way over there every other day, if not every day. Lord! I wish I had my own hospital, here in the village!'

'It would be gorgeous, wouldn't it! How big would you want it to be?'

'Oh, about fifty beds. I'd have the laboratory –' He pulled an envelope out of his pocket, unscrewed his fountain pen, and began to make a rough sketch. 'The lab would be here – the X-ray room *here* – and the operating room –' His voice went on, cheerful now, as he became absorbed in his dream hospital.

Sue leaned forward, her hair brushing his cheek. Neither heard Mrs. Cooney in the doorway, or knew that, seeing the two heads close together over the envelope, she had gone away very quietly, smiling.

It was late when Bill left, and Sue didn't know until next day that he had driven home in darkness – because he had found both his headlights smashed when he came out of the house.

7

Mr. Todd

'WHAT do you think, Mrs. Cooney?'

'I dunno. It's all of a passel with the other things that's gone on – windows broke – tyres cut. Kinder senseless, the hull thing. Mebbe that's something to foller up.'

'How do you mean?'

Mrs. Cooney didn't reply at once, being engaged in putting wood ashes into a flannel bag. She was making a weak solution of lye for use in hulling corn; there would be succotash for dinner tomorrow night – succotash made as it was made three hundred years ago.

Sue watched, fascinated. She had wedged herself into the chimney, on the shelf formed by the Dutch oven – now used as a receptacle for paper bags and back numbers of the *Almanac*. The chimney shadow deepened Sue's hair to copper. Her silk-clad legs dangled against a seventeenth-century oven door. Outside, great blue cloud shadows drifted across the snow-covered hills.

Mrs. Cooney put the last spoonful of ash into the bag, pulled the drawstring tight, and said, 'Whoever's after the doctor is spiteful and not very bright, I sh'd say. Mightn't be a bad idea to look for some such critter.'

Sue straightened up. 'Mrs. Cooney! Suppose –'

'Wisht ye wouldn't call me Mrs. Cooney. We'd oughter be past the how-de-do stage. My friends call me Veazie Ann.'

The name no longer seemed funny to Sue. 'I'd love to, Veazie Ann,' she said.

'That's better. Now what was ye goin' to say?'

'I was going to say – would it be a good idea if I did a little private sleuthing along that line? I mean, Bill's so busy he hasn't time to hunt down every little detail. There *might* be something he overlooked.'

Veazie Ann plopped the flannel bag into an enormous kettle of water. 'I ain't so sure it is a good notion. Right now ye got no special place in the community and folks here like things to be kind of ordered and in set places. You're a stranger. Folks don't know ye, yet. If you was the town nurse 'twould be diff-runt. 'Twould be part of your job, then.'

'I see. I suppose I'd better drop the whole thing – for now.'

'Seems's though. Suz! There's that tarnation phone! Run and answer it like a good girl, will ye?'

Lot Phinney's thin old voice came over the wire. 'Elias Todd's back,' he said tartly. 'Better git to him while th' gittin's good.'

Sue was pale with excitement when she returned to the kitchen. Veazie Ann glanced at her, startled.

'Land, child! What's happened?'

'Elias Todd!'

'You don't say,' remarked Veazie Ann calmly. 'Well, there's no call to be scairt. Put on that little green sport dress with the white collar and cuffs, and wear that mite of a fur hat with your black coat – the one with the stand-up collar. Better take my old car. If it'll start it'll jack-rabbit ye there all right.'

'Should I telephone him first?'

'No. Somebody'd put ye off. They can't hardly make out the diffrunce between Todd and God over at the Inn.'

The old car did start, and Sue bounced up the winding road to Bald Trail Inn in a combined state of panic and determination.

'It's my last chance!' she told herself, over and over again.

Elias Todd, when favouring the town with his presence, lived in a suite of rooms at the Inn. It was a luxurious inn, built to attract wealthy ski enthusiasts, and its exterior of logs and stone did not in the least conceal its expensiveness.

The uniformed desk clerk stated with polite finality that Mr. Todd was inspecting his kennels and could not be disturbed. Who should he say called?

Sue gave him her name and said that she would return later. She had, however, no intention of returning later. She was going to see Mr. Todd now.

Apparently it never occurred to the desk clerk that any one would have the temerity to go and look for the August Presence, and Sue went on her way without hindrance.

She picked her way across the wide verandah through laughing groups of men and girls in bright ski costumes, and went round to the side of the building. Anyone on the verandah could undoubtedly have directed her to the kennels, but she had a sudden longing to hear a native voice and see a calm, unimpressed native face. She found what she sought in the person of a carpenter who was repairing weather stripping on a sun-porch door.

'Yup,' he drawled. 'Kennels is jest over there beyond th' rise. Can't miss 'em. Look like a fenced-in auto camp an' sound like Tophet on th' Judgement Day. All flummoxed up, they be – to keep them critters happy. . . . Todd's there.'

Sue approached the kennels through a din of barking and laughed in spite of her nervousness as a coated battalion of dachshunds rushed to the wire fence in a phalanx spiked with tails.

She found the owner in the kennels office.

He was not unlike her idea of him – a well-groomed, heavily built man of about fifty with a colourless face and pouches under his eyes. He was not at all displeased at being confronted by a pretty girl, and one of his square soft hands closed on Sue's arm as he offered her a chair. It was not a very decided clasp, however, and when Sue withdrew her arm he made no further attempt to touch her, but sat down at his desk with an important cough.

'What can I do for you?' he said.

Sue waited a moment, until the uproar of barking outside began to diminish. She was seated facing him and looked far more at ease than she felt. She wished he would say or do something which would give her a clue as to how to begin, but he said nothing; his only move was to light a cigar.

'Mr. Todd,' Sue began, 'I'm Springdale's Visiting Nurse – at least, I'm going to be if somebody will help a little.' She paused, wondering if this were a wrong start. Mr. Todd waited, watching her through a blue cloud of cigar smoke. She thought, 'He's very cagey. I'll just have to go ahead – and I'd better not try to be funny.'

She told her story simply, sticking to facts, stating her situation, her purpose and qualifications, the probability of aid from the Red Cross. She stressed the need of a purely local Visiting Nurse. Mr. Todd said nothing in an aroma of bay rum, tweed, and cigar smoke. His expression was one of such exaggerated shrewdness – the eyes narrowed, lips drawn down – that Sue wondered if he had practised looking like that before a mirror. If he had, she thought, he ought to practise some more.

She finished by saying that the townspeople would be extremely grateful for the institution of a Public Health Nurse – that only lack of funds had prevented their giving her a job.

'Mm,' said Mr. Todd, and drummed on the desk with his pudgy fingers. Then he took the cigar out of his mouth and said abruptly, 'You want me to pay your salary – is that it?'

'Yes.' Sue's hands tightened over her handbag.

'How much salary would you want?'

'A hundred and twenty-five dollars a month is the usual beginning salary for a Visiting Nurse.' Sue was making a desperate effort to remain composed. He was going to do it! He must be going to! Actually!

'And what do I get out of it?'

'I – you get a chance to do something very real for the good of the community,' she said, and knew that she sounded unconvincing.

'Mm,' said Mr. Todd again. His glance travelled over Sue from trim ankles to black astrakhan cap. 'That's all very idealistic, Miss Barton, but you are mistaken in thinking that people with money can afford to go into every casual venture that offers. A great many people make that mistake.' His eyes were suddenly complacent. 'You have no idea how many begging letters I get every day.'

Sue's face was crimson.

'I'm not begging, Mr. Todd,' she said evenly, 'and this is not a casual venture. You will get a large return for your money.'

'Such as?'

'A great improvement in public health conditions – which is surely worth while – and the gratitude of the townspeople, which ought to be excellent advertising for you as owner of this inn.'

'Public gratitude, Miss Barton, is very uncertain, and as for the improvement in conditions – that depends upon you and this young doctor. I know nothing of either of you.' His tone was not unkind; it was flat with finality.

Sue swallowed. 'You can easily find out about us both, Mr. Todd. Dr. Barry has a brilliant record, and I assure you that I am perfectly capable of handling my end of the work. If it's a question of money alone I think that, once I get started, the ordinary monthly fees of a Visiting Nurse will make up a large percentage of my salary.'

'Do you guarantee that?'

'Well – no. But –'

'I thought not. I'm afraid you're a little too ready to make rash statements.' He smiled at her from the heights. 'You have plenty of nerve, Miss Barton. And that, I may say, doesn't inspire me with great confidence. I would not object to improving the local health conditions under the right circumstances, but they must be right. All my life my unfailingly successful rule has been' – he cleared his throat – 'never to go into anything which isn't sure, or in which there are definitely unknown factors. I have applied this rule to small matters as well as large, and I see no reason for breaking that rule now.'

Sue looked at him in sincere bewilderment. 'I don't understand,' she said. 'What's uncertain or unknown in this, Mr. Todd?'

T—C

'You are, Miss Barton.'

'I?'

'Certainly. The fact that you have plunged into this, attempting to achieve something which, on the face of it, is highly improbable of success, shows a very youthful lack of judgement.'

Sue longed to hurl something at him – anything to shatter that combined expression of caution and self-righteousness.

'Why?' she said.

Mr. Todd erupted cigar smoke. 'You have not been sure of anything in this situation, but you have gone ahead regardless. I grant that your training seems to have been excellent, but on your own statement you have always worked under the guidance of competent organizations. You have no record of independent achievement.'

'But –'

'I can respect achievement as well as the next man, but so far you have not been able even to achieve your present purpose. I am not going to spend money, or risk my reputation for good judgement, on a pretty child who rushes into wild uncertainties. I cannot employ people like that in positions of responsibility.'

Sue forced herself to speak pleasantly. 'But Mr. Todd, you're saying that I cannot be an independent Visiting Nurse until I have been an independent Visiting Nurse. That's hardly reasonable.'

'It's my considered opinion. I'm sorry, Miss Barton.'

Sue gathered up gloves and bag and rose, too outraged to heed the sinking feeling in the pit of her stomach. She wanted to say, 'Oh, yes! You're so sorry you can hardly stand it!' But she remembered Bill. Mr. Todd was influential in spite of the fact that the townspeople laughed at him. If she antagonized him there was no knowing how it might affect Bill, or his practice. And so, holding out her hand, she said quietly, 'Thank you, Mr. Todd.'

Mr. Todd patted her hand – cautiously – and Sue would

have given a good deal to cry sharply, 'Look out!' He would almost certainly have gone over backwards in his chair.

'Oh, not at all, not at all!' said Mr. Todd as if he had been showering her with blessings. He rose and opened the door for her. Perhaps he felt a stirring of compunction as he looked at her lifted chin, for he remarked suddenly, 'I'm sorry if I have seemed harsh, Miss Barton. I hope you will have better luck another time.'

'Thank you,' said Sue again. 'Oh, *goodness*!' There was an agonized yelp as she stepped through the door, and a small plump dachshund fled from under her feet, holding up his forepaw. Distressed, Sue dropped to one knee on the doorstep and held out her hand. '*Please*, excuse me, darling!' she cried. 'I didn't mean it – truly!'

The martyred dachshund fled to Mr. Todd, who picked him up with soothing words.

Sue rose, feeling that she had added the one touch needed to make a bad impression worse – not that it mattered now. 'Good day, Mr. Todd.' Then to the dachshund, 'Good-bye, little man. I'm awfully sorry.'

Snow squeaked underfoot. The chorus of barks grew faint. Sue climbed into Veazie Ann's old car and drove away. She didn't trouble to back round and head down the mountain, but followed the road up. She would go back to Veazie Ann and Bill after a while and tell them that she had failed – but not yet. Please – not yet!'

The car laboured and panted, but it was sturdy in spite of its years and it carried her on up. The curves and the more slippery spots in the road had been sanded to reduce the danger of skidding. She was unaware of the car's efforts, unaware of the chilly smoothness of the wheel. For the first time since she had come to Springdale she failed to see the panorama of sky and peaks and cloud shadows.

'I won't cry,' she told herself. 'I won't! There's no use!'

It was all so hopeless. There was no point in blaming Elias Todd. She had managed him badly, and it was her fault that he had not understood. Probably there was a good deal in what he had said. After all, he *didn't* know her, and his caution was something he couldn't help. But what now? Back home to stay with her family? Back to Henry Street? Private nursing? Hospital work? To each of these possibilities every spark of obstinacy in Sue flared 'NO!' But it would have to be one of them. There wasn't anything else.

The car struggled on with increasing difficulty until at last Sue realized that here there was no sand. A driveway into a farmhouse offered a chance to turn. Sue backed in, but once the car was facing down the mountain she shut off the ignition and got out. Perhaps just looking at the hills would help. They were so quiet – so lovely – so old and undisturbed.

She brushed the snow off a rock and sat down. How long she sat there she never knew. She had lost all sense of the passage of time, and the sound of a voice behind her gave her a painful start.

'Sightly, ain't it?' said the voice.

Sue turned.

The speaker was a tall, wiry, farm woman with greying sandy hair, weather-wrinkled face, and hawk nose. She had thrown a man's coat over her shoulders and held it round her against the icy wind while she looked at Sue with bright, inquiring eyes.

'Be you all right?' she asked. 'You been a settin' there so long I got kinder worried. See ye frum th' winder. I hollered a couple of times but you never said nothing, so I come on out. Ain't you nigh froze to death?'

Sue found her voice, and in the same moment became aware that she was so numb with cold she could scarcely move.

'I – g-g-guess I am,' she said through chattering teeth. 'I w-was th-thinking and d-d-didn't notice.'

'Land of liberty! Well, you come right in the house and I'll fix ye a good hot toddy.'

She went ahead of Sue, still talking, up the path to the kitchen door. Sue followed numbly.

The toddy was good and it was hot. It was also very strong. As warmth returned to Sue's body optimism took the place of her despair. Perhaps there was still a chance — if she could find it.

Sue's hostess bustled round the sunny kitchen with nervous, determined movements. She set out johnny-cake, home-made butter, doughnuts. She shook up the fire. She put coffee on to boil. Her name, she said, looking at Sue with kindly curiosity, was Edgett — Martha Edgett. She was a widow, and, Sue thought, looking out at the substantial barns and the acres tilted against the sky, a very well-to-do widow. She said that it was difficult to run a farm with nothing but hired men. She said that her relations wanted her to move down to the village, but she couldn't seem to. She'd lived all her life here and 'twarn't as if she had nothing to do, like some. There was the farm to manage, and then her club work took up a lot of time.

'What kind of a club?' Sue inquired, more out of politeness than curiosity.

'It's a Farm Club.' Mrs. Edgett whisked away the empty toddy glass, replacing it with a cup of hot coffee, and sat down with a jerk. 'We're consolidated,' she said. 'There's a branch in each of the villages around.'

'What do you do? Sew?'

'Sartinly not! We git people to come and lecture an' teach us how to do a lot of useful things we didn't know — like caning chairs and things. We're a tryin' to improve things around. Somebody'd ought to, an' the men-folks wun't never git to it.'

Sue straightened in her chair, her eyes shining.

'Mrs. Edgett, have you ever thought how much a local Visiting Nurse could do for your community?'

'I dunno's I have. Why? Be you a nurse?'

'Yes, I am. My name is Barton — Sue Barton. I'm engaged to Dr. Barry down in the village — and I'd like to tell you a story if I may.'

Sue told it well, for the hot toddy had revived her spirits.

She began with her arrival at home to prepare for her wedding – and went on from there, inclusive of Mr. Todd. She sketched her background and her training. She explained her hopes. She told of the possibility of aid from the Red Cross.

Mrs. Edgett listened, nodding from time to time, her eyes sharp points of intelligence. Once she said, 'You poor young ones!' And when Sue had finished she began to ask questions. Sue answered them clearly.

'Well,' Mrs. Edgett said at last, 'as I see it, you need a hundred and twenty-five dollars a month, a car, and supplies. You figger the Red Cross would furnish them last, and I shouldn't wonder if you *could* make up a good deal of your salary. It could go into a fund. Ye'd expect to do a lot for the wimmin, I suppose?'

'Oh yes.' Sue described the Henry Street Mothers' Clubs.

'Ayuh. That's same as the State Nurses does, only it's kinder hard for 'em to git away off up here – especially in winter.'

'I know.'

'Ye'd go wherever and whenever ye was needed, same's th' State Nurses, chargin' only them as could pay?'

'Of course.'

There was a long pause. Then Mrs. Edgett said calmly, 'Well, I guess ye got a job.'

It was too sudden. A lump rose in Sue's throat, choking her.

'But Mrs. Edgett,' she managed to say, 'are you sure the Club would be willing? Could they manage the –'

'The money? Not th' Springdale Club alone. But all of 'em together could. There's five villages right in th' neighbour-hood. Of course th' Red Cross'll have to help – and ye'd have to tend th' Club members free. 'Twould be a real good thing – git us a lot of new members – an' I'll hist up their dues a mite to pay for it.'

'But would the Club be willing?'

'Sakes alive, child! We ain't fools! There's a cryin' need for just such a thing – and with th' Club back of ye th' Red Cross had ought to be willin'. What's more I'm president of th' hull consolidation, an' if I'm a backin' ye there wun't be no opposition to speak of.'

This last seemed more than probable to the staggered Sue.

'Then – you don't think – I'm too young – or rash – or have bad judgement – or – or anything?'

'Ye got to be young to do sech work. Old bones can't stand it. Ye got good trainin'. I'll have to check on all ye told me, you understand, so's to have it all straight fer th' Club. But *I* know ye're all right. I been a watchin' ye. Ye're a real pretty girl, but ye don't do no monkey-shines a drorin' attention to it. Ye talk straight, stickin' to facts an' not tryin' to bamboozle me. That shows ye're sensible an' got a clear head. Ye ain't criticized Elias Todd. That shows ye're a lady. Ye come straight out about bein' engaged to the doctor, saying' half what ye want's to be near him – as ye should be in his trouble. So I know ye're honest an' loyal. Land, child! *Don't do that!*'

Sue's eyes had filled with tears of happiness and gratitude. She laughed shakily, unable to speak.

'Sho, now,' said Mrs. Edgett. 'What's more,' she added, 'if it comes to judgement an' rashness – anybody that ain't got sperit enough to git after what they want ain't a goin' to git much that's wuth while – as Elias Todd would of found out long ago, if he'd had th' gumption to git him a wife. If ever I see a man needed a smart woman to snatch him bald-headed, he's it – fer all his money! It's all I can do, every time I lookit him, to keep from tellin' him what for an' never mind why!'

Sue really laughed this time. 'Y-you're a darling, Mrs. Edgett. 'I – I don't know how to thank you!'

The wiry figure leaned across the table to pat Sue on the shoulder. 'Shouldn't wonder,' Mrs. Edgett said, 'if 'twould be us'll be doin' th' thankin'.'

8

Undercurrents

SUE had always been a sensible driver, but no one who witnessed her descent of the mountain that day would have believed it. Mrs. Cooney's car plunged downward in leaps and bounds, galloping between walls of snow like an old plough horse. Sue rocked behind the wheel and gazed down upon the toy roofs of the village with affectionate eyes. Even the frozen lake and its dam – once a source of water power for a mill long since demolished – seemed especially hers.

Mrs. Edgett was to lay the Visiting Nurse project before the Farm Club the next day, and she had said that she would attend to the application for help from the Red Cross – which meant that it was as good as done. 'Golly, I'm so happy!' Sue murmured to the little car.

She drove straight to Bill's tiny surgery, praying that he would not be busy. But he was. Her news must wait. She went on through town and up the climbing road to the grey-shingled little house, thinking how she would tell Veazie Ann. She would come in soberly, and Veazie Ann would glance at her face and say, 'So!' and 'Don't take it to heart, child!' And Sue would take off her hat and coat, very slowly, and go and sit down, and say, 'Are you *sure*, Veazie Ann, that you won't mind having Marianna here?' Then she would grin like anything, and Veazie Ann would stare at that triumphant grin and say, 'You – you don't mean to *tell* me –' And Sue would nod, very self-possessed and calm.

The barn door had been left open for her. Sue drove in with appropriate sedateness, climbed out of the car, and went through the back room to the kitchen – her face carefully blank, her steps slow.

Veazie Ann was 'into the oven' as usual, testing a pudding

with a broom straw. Sue closed the kitchen door with funereal
care and waited. Veazie Ann withdrew the straw and examined
it. She had not yet turned to look at Sue when she remarked over
her shoulder:

'So ye done it!'

Sue's jaw dropped. 'Wha –' she began. 'Oh, Veazie Ann –
who told you?'

'You did, child.'

'*I* did?'

'Sartin',' said Veazie Ann indulgently. 'Ye come in slow, but
your steps was lighter'n I ever heard 'em – which is sayin'
a good deal. And ye stood there behind me a breathin' quick
and soft. Folks that's miserable breathes slow and deep, like
they needed a lot of air to hold 'em up.'

'Heavens!' said Sue. 'Can I get you a job as a detective, or
would you rather take over Scotland Yard? Oh, Veazie Ann!'
Sue twirled on her toes, skirts flying, all her self-possession forgotten. 'Oh, Veazie Ann! Isn't it gorgeous? Isn't it marvellous? Isn't it heavenly?'

' 'Tain't onsatisfactory,' said Veazie Ann. 'But how come
you got round Elias so quick?'

'I didn't. He turned me down cold. He acted as if I was a
cross between a Persian cat and a War Menace.'

'Then ye *didn't* get the job!'

'Oh yes, I did!'

Veazie Ann was startled enough this time to satisfy even
Sue's craving for a dramatic reception of her news.

'Land of Goshen!' she said. 'Will ye set down and tell me
what's it all about?'

Sue told her, but not sitting down. She couldn't have remained quiet in one spot. It was Veazie Ann who sat, the
broom straw forgotten in one hand, a kitchen towel in the
other. 'Stars alive!' she said. 'I never thought of the Farm
Club. I b'long to it myself, too. But Martha Edgett's the
Grand Panjandrum. If she's for ye, there ain't no question.
My land! The doctor'll have a conniption. He's been awful

blue, poor soul, a lookin' for ye to go back home any minute. Whyn't ye telephone him now?'

'It's right in the middle of his surgery hours. I did go by there, hoping, but he had patients. You can't interrupt a doctor when he's working.'

'I s'pose not,' said Veazie Ann dryly, 'not even if the skies was to fall – and it was only an ingrowin' hair. Well, he's comin' to supper. Shouldn't wonder if he got here early. He rang ye this mornin', after you'd left, and I told him where ye'd gone.'

'Did he say anything about – I mean, has anything else happened – like the smashed headlights?'

'He didn't say. He wouldn't over the phone – with Mary Tinney all ears. Ye can hear her gum a cracklin' all the time ye're talkin'. Seems's if we might have an operator oncet that gum gives her a toothache.'

Sue laughed. 'Is *that* what it is? I thought it was static electricity or a bad connection.' She glanced at the clock. 'Goodness! I'd no idea it was so late! I've been gone nearly all day. Golly! I wish he'd come!'

He came, as Veazie Ann had predicted, early.

Sue heard the car and was at the door in a single bound, face glowing, slender figure tense with excitement. There would be no pretended failure this time. Bill must know at once.

He was slow in getting out of the car, and once out he paused to close a window, and then stood motionless in the dusk, staring down the valley at the mountains. Sue had been poised to call him, but something in the way he stood silenced her. The winter twilight blurred outlines, but she could see clearly enough to note the way his shoulders sagged, and that when he turned towards the house his movements were heavy.

In another moment he had seen her and squared his shoulders as he hurried across the snow-banked driveway. When he stepped into the light from the doorway he smiled at

Sue – a smile of reassurance and support, a gay smile that was
belied by the shadow in his eyes.

Sue cried, 'But I got it! Everything's all right, Bill!'

He stopped short. 'Good Lord! You *got* it?' He seemed
dazed.

'Well, if I didn't you'd better try to get me away quietly.
Would you come in, Dr. Barry, or shall I tell you about it by
frozen stages out here? We *could* run over to the top of Mount
Washington if you prefer. A good two-hundred-mile-an-hour
wind might –'

He swept her into his arms and across the threshold into the
kitchen, where he dumped her, laughing, on Veazie Ann's
lap.

'Suz!' said Veazie Ann.

Bill stood over them. 'Come on – give!'

Sue scrambled to her feet and retreated to the wood box.
He was frightfully tired, she saw. He must have had a hard
day. There were lines round his eyes and he was pale in spite
of the great news – though his pallor grew less as he watched
Sue. It was almost as if he drew renewed strength from her
vitality.

'Sit down!' said Sue firmly.

Bill threw off his coat and sat, with an unconscious sigh of
weariness, though his face was eager. As Sue told her story with
all its dramatic details she noticed that his hand went to his
moustache from time to time, with that reflective, puzzled
gesture. Something else was troubling him, she was certain.

She didn't learn what it was, however, until after supper,
when Veazie Ann had left them together in the front room.
Then it came out. He had lost a patient, early that morning.
The call had come before dawn – and three hours too late to
save a baby in convulsions from whooping-cough.

'I don't see why they didn't call me sooner,' he said. 'They've
been good patients of mine for two years and I did a peach of a
job on the oldest boy's broken arm. But I had a feeling that they
didn't want to call me – that they didn't trust me. It wasn't

anything you could put your finger on – just something in the atmosphere. And the baby – died – because they didn't call me in time.'

'I suppose they blamed you for it?' Sue spoke from the depths of experience.

'Probably.'

Sue laid her hand over his. 'I'm sorry, darling – awfully.'

Bill stirred in his chair. 'I'll be glad when you can start working with me.'

'So will I! I wonder when I can begin?'

She began within four days – but the wait was too well filled with events to seem long.

First, there was the meeting of the Farm Clubs, which Sue, naturally, did not attend. But Veazie Ann did, returning with the report that the idea of a Rural Nurse had been greeted with enthusiasm. There had been some demur in regard to Sue's salary, but Mrs. Edgett had carried the day. A Visiting Nurse Committee had been appointed, with Mrs. Edgett as chairman. Sue's monthly reports were to go to this committee, by way of Mrs. Edgett. And it was Mrs. Edgett who telephoned the State Red Cross Headquarters the following day.

The Red Cross was co-operative, unofficially, but said that the application for a car and medical supplies must go through the usual channels – which might require two weeks or more.

A committee meeting was next – held in an anteroom of the town hall. Sue was invited to this in order that she might meet the members and tell them about her work at Henry Street. She found it a simple matter, for the State Visiting Nurse Association had followed the Henry Street plan, and every village had received benefits from the State Nurses, either in schools or in homes. The work they were doing was understood and appreciated, and Sue didn't have to go into complicated details.

Bill, too, had been asked to the meeting, and was promptly appointed Medical Adviser to the committee. He had to leave early, but he stayed long enough to hear Sue launched on her speech, and upset her gravity completely by turning at the door to make a horrible face at her.

On her way home from the meeting Sue encountered Ira Prouty.

'How's your hand?' she asked at once.

'Fine!' he said heartily. 'Never had no trouble from it after the one day. Hear you're a goin' to be our Visiting Nurse.'

'How did you know?'

' 'Tain't no secret. There's a notice frum Martha Edgett stuck up in th' Pust office, tellin' all about it, an Lot Phinney's been spreadin' himself. Come right out an' told two people. Never knew Lot to be so plumb enthusiastic. Even said it might be a good thing.'

'He's been a darling.'

Ira grinned. 'Dunno's any of us ever thought of him in jest *that* way.' He paused, sobering, and seemed on the verge of an important pronouncement, but apparently he thought better of it, for after a moment he went on his way, remarking only, 'If so be I can help ye any time, I'll be glad to.'

Sue wondered what he had meant to say – and then forgot about the matter, for tomorrow she was to go with Bill on his rounds. She couldn't, of course, continue to go with him, once she was established, for she would have her own work to do. But Mrs. Edgett had said that Sue might as well start getting acquainted with conditions generally, and the thought of returning to work – especially with Bill – dimmed all minor considerations.

Before Sue went to bed that night she wrote to her mother, telling her all that had happened. A letter also went to Kit and Marianna, which ended with the suggestion that Marianna should come to Springdale. This last required tact, for Marianna had a very stubborn pride. In New York she had been earning a living. She had contributed as much as she could to the expenses, and she had done most of the housework. In Springdale, she could help Veazie Ann, after school, but she would not be earning. Marianna would balk at that – unless she could be persuaded that Sue needed her. So the letter complained of loneliness, and ended with the statement that Sue felt it was a good deal to ask, but she did wish Marianna would come to Springdale – thought, of course, if she didn't *want* to –

Kit would read between the lines and urge Marianna to come.

'So that's all fixed,' Sue thought as she got into bed. 'I wonder what Ira Prouty meant to say to me – and didn't?'

9

Tea

BILL came for her at nine in the morning, his car in a high state of polish, and a long amiable bellow from the horn brought Sue out. Her blue uniform crackled starchily under the cloth coat which must do until she could get a raccoon coat to keep out the mountain winds. Her Henry Street bag was heavy on her arm once more.

Bill sprang out to open the car door for her, his face glowing. He was completely unaware of Veazie Ann in the kitchen window, or of anything except shadowed red curls under a black felt hat brim, and a vivid young face with warm mouth and steady eyes.

'Taxi, lady?' he said, bowing from the waist. 'Takes you anywhere – gentle as a mule – kicks women and children first – has Roman bath, nickel-plated bar, and special mortgage!'

Sue paused, clasping mittened hands, her expression instantly and utterly imbecilic. 'A mortgage?' she cried .'How romantic! A little, rose-covered, vine-clad mortgage! Oh, *doctor!*'

Her imitation of a gushing woman patient was perfect.

'Madam!' said Bill sternly. 'My heart is in the Highlands and –'

'Your feet are in a snowdrift. You'll get a snivelling cold.'

'The woman has no soul whatever. Ah, well! Get in, Miss Barton! Get in! I'll try to bear with you.'

They drove away, laughing, for their first day's work together in Springdale.

It was not the kind of day that Sue had expected in view of the fact that Bill was the only doctor within a radius of twenty-five miles of farms and villages. Sue had thought that he would be rushed with work.

The first visit was to the typhoid patients – the little girl and her grandmother – a routine visit, for both patients were doing well. Mrs. Mason, the child's mother, had been instructed by one of the State Nurses and had done the nursing and done it capably, but she was eager for another practical demonstration of a bed bath.

Bill seemed in no hurry, and waited without impatience while Sue gave the bath and showed the woman how to change the undersheet, moving the patient once to the edge of the bed, and then back over the folds of the fresh sheet.

Sue wondered, as she worked, about the advisability of charging for this visit. Was it supposed to be a regular visit, or was it just an introductory call with Bill? In her excitement at starting work she hadn't thought to ask him what he had told the Masons about Visiting Nurses' fees, and since she had come with him and he had introduced her to the family, she hadn't followed the usual Henry Street method with new cases.

At Henry Street the Visiting Nurse, after introducing herself, and while she lays out the necessary equipment, explains the nursing service and the charge for it. If the patient is unable to pay there is no charge. But now Sue felt that she wasn't making quite a regular visit.

The problem was solved for her. When she finished the bath and bed-making young Mrs. Mason handed her a dollar and a half and said shyly, 'Th' doctor told me this was the price. It don't seem much for what you done.' She added unexpectedly, 'We think a lot of the doctor. An' I don't care what anybody says – he's done just fine for *us*.'

Sue was startled for a moment by this cryptic remark. Then she thought, 'Nonsense! It didn't mean anything. It's just her way of speaking.'

On the way to the next case Sue told Bill of her dilemma about the fee.

'Of course you should charge for it,' he said. 'You're working on the Farm Club's time from today. I explained to the family – but you don't charge the next case because the people have no money. I don't charge them either.'

The next patient was a man whose foot had been injured by a falling rock. Sue was to do the dressing daily. From here they went on to a chronic heart case, an old lady whose daughter wanted instruction in home-nursing. This ended the visits in Springdale.

Sue thought it a little odd, but she made no comment, telling herself that any doctor has dull days.

'We've got just time for a visit in Harville before lunch,' Bill said as they left the house. 'I've got a bad case of 'flu there. You won't be able to make visits in Harville by yourself until you get your car, but I want you to see the village. It needs a lot of what you've got.'

Harville was back in the hills about five miles from Springdale, over a narrow, winding road, and the car made slow progress. As it crept up the hills and slid down to the valleys Bill talked and Sue listened, watching him.

In spite of her interest in what he was saying she couldn't help being aware of his nearness – of the blocked line from his dark head to his solidly set shoulders. His strong face and high forehead, framed by the car window, were outlined against the hills. His long, supple hands manoeuvred the car over the road with casual skill.

'New Hampshire is a healthy state,' he was saying. 'Most of the diseases are those of late middle-life or old age – heart disease, cancer, and so on. What the people need most is education in hygiene, and that's difficult – with the population so scattered. Whooping-cough is the worst of the children's diseases. I really have more work in emergencies than anything else.' He turned to smile at her, slim and vivid beside him.

'What kind of emergencies?' Sue asked, suddenly realizing that a mountain or country district must have its own particular accidents.

'Well, there are ski-ing accidents in winter – broken bones, mostly. There are more axe cuts in winter, and more people hurt by having logs fall on them. In spring you get the near-drownings and the brush-fire burns.'

'Doesn't anybody care to break through the ice in winter?'

'Don't be a dope, my sweet. Ice comes thick and fast up here.'

'Oh yes. I forgot. Well, go on – what happens to cheer everybody up in summer?'

'Plenty, poor devils! They get gored by bulls; horses kick them; stones fall on them; they run pitchforks into themselves; they get cramps swimming, and hernias from lifting. There are difficulties with porcupine quills, too, and snake bite, and all the summer people get poison ivy.'

'How about autumn?'

'Trees.'

'What *are* you talking about?'

'Apple time, darling. When people fall out of trees and off ladders. They start repairing roofs, too, and fall off those, and down wells.'

Sue glanced at him sideways. 'Just the *fall* of the year,' she said faintly.

Bill leapt behind the wheel. 'I *won't* marry a woman who makes puns – even good ones, if there are any – and that's about the worst one I ever heard.'

'Oh!' Sue wailed in mock terror, shrinking back. 'I'll be good!'

Bill leaned over and kissed her so swiftly that the car had no time to change its direction.

'That's for you!' he said. 'Take it and like it!'

'I do. But would you please tell me why people should fall down wells in the – autumn – more than other times?'

'Because that's the season wells are low and can be cleaned out. Look, darling! There's Harville.' He stopped the car.

Sue looked. 'Goodness!' she cried. 'How awful!'

The village of Harville lay below them in a cuplike depression in the hills – twenty or thirty houses, unpainted and ramshackle. Many of them were literally falling down. Ends were open to the weather; there were great holes in the roofs, bulging cracks in the walls, broken window-panes stuffed with old rags or paper. Picket fences lay rotting on the ground among fragments of cars, tin cans, and rusty farm machinery.

The place was an ugly black sore on the clean flank of the mountain.

Sue stared at it, aghast. She had seen wretched living conditions in the city slums, but there the people could do nothing about it. Here, surely, even a child with a hammer and a few pieces of tin could improve matters. There was other material, too. The mountains were covered with timber on the lower slopes, and stream beds were piled with rocks. The timber might belong to some lumber company and could not be cut, but the stones were certainly free to everyone. Sue thought that even she could have built a snug shelter with the materials at hand.

'But why?' she said to Bill. 'They don't *have* to live so wretchedly here. And they can't like it.'

Bill sat looking down at the sagging roofs and exposed beams. 'No,' he said. 'They don't have to – in one sense – and they don't like it.'

'Then why?'

'They haven't the energy, nor the initiative that comes from energy. They manage to fill their stomachs with food – of sorts – but it's food that doesn't give them anything. It doesn't build them up – it runs them down. They're tired all the time – and when you're tired you don't care. You can't.'

'But there must be some with vitality.'

'Yes – they're the ones who get away as quickly and as young as possible. It's easy for us to call them shiftless and not bother with them. We've never known that kind of tiredness in all our lives. We've never known the hopelessness that comes from continual failure. That's horrible, you know – to fail at everything and not really know why.'

Sue glanced at him. He really cared about Harville – was almost bitter about it.

'They resist efforts to help them,' he went on, 'because they can't see ahead. They don't believe anything will really help so they just don't try – and they wish we wouldn't bother them.'

'I see what you mean. It's as if they were shut in a cage until they lost the use of their arms and legs and then somebody came along and said brightly, "Brace up and do some hard work and you'll be fine." '

'That's it exactly! The thing people like us don't realize is that it is hard work for them just to be alive. The State Nurses are in despair over the place. They can't get here often, and when they do come the people don't respond. I've been in hopes – with you here close at hand – that you might get somewhere with them. It'll take a long time – two or three years, probably – and their first impression of you will be important.'

'What should I do?'

'The only thing you can possibly do is make them like you, for now. You can build on that by degrees.'

He slipped the car into gear and they went on down. The village had no streets. The houses were scattered over the slopes and the road wound casually among them. Bill stopped the car before a leaning shanty and got out, taking Sue's bag and his own.

'You'll get a shock when you see Mrs. Leffert,' he said. 'She's thirty – and she looks fifty.'

The path to the door was icy, and Sue was grateful for the iron strength in Bill's arm, holding her on her feet. She was feeling very nervous and uncertain, now that she realized that so much was expected of her. Her heart sank further when the door was opened by a sallow, wrinkled scrap of a woman with greasy hair and hollow eyes. The woman stood aside without comment while they entered, nodding indifferently as Bill introduced Sue. This was going to be very difficult, Sue thought. Indifference was far worse to combat than resentment.

The shanty had two rooms – the first a filthy kitchen crammed with odds and ends of broken furniture, rags, rusted pots and pans, and a decrepit stove, which gave off a stifling heat.

The table was littered with dirty, chipped dishes. A teapot with broken snout occupied a chair, its thick brew evidently days old. A baby and three young children stared from a corner.

The adjoining room held a vast feather bed with the patient in it, and was further embellished by a chair and a rough table. But this room was fairly clean and the walls had been papered with newspapers to keep out the wind that whistled through the gaping cracks. The newspapers were fresh, and Sue guessed that Bill had not only brought them, but tacked them up himself.

The patient lay in a miserable heap in the depths of the bed, his face flushed with fever. Bill approached him with a simple, concerned friendliness and a complete absence of 'bed-side manner'.

'How are you, Jim?' he said, and Sue stood waiting, wondering what she ought to do – what would be the right move under the circumstances. Her mind was a terrifying blank.

'Not so bad, Doc,' the man said, in reply to Bill's question. 'I slep' most all night.'

'That's good,' Bill said, pleased. 'Jim, this is Miss Barton, the Visiting Nurse. Miss Barton – Mr. Leffert. I want her to give you an alcohol rub, Jim.'

The man nodded indifferently, as his wife had done. His eyes followed Bill. Sue had meant to smile and say something friendly, but it didn't seem to matter whether she did or not. How she was to make people like this become aware of her sufficiently to like her she didn't know. Certainly she could do nothing in one visit. She set about her work without a word.

Mrs. Leffert shuffled to the door when Sue was half-way through the alcohol rub.

'Doc,' the woman said heavily, 'Ezra Torrey's boy is down with sumpthin'. He wants you should come up there.'

'All right. I'll go now, while Jim is being fixed up.' He was gone with the words.

Sue worked on, swiftly and quietly, and saw the lines of discomfort smooth, little by little, from the man's face. Once she said, 'That's better.' He made no reply.

She could hear occasional shufflings in the next room and now and then a squeak from the baby. There was no other sound except the whistle of wind round the shanty.

Then Mrs. Leffert's scream tore open the silence! Agonized screams from the baby followed it.

Sue flung the bedcovers over her patient and dashed for the kitchen.

Mrs. Leffert was kneeling on the floor beside the baby, frantically scooping hot coals out of its clothing with her bare hands, while the older children clung together in the corner.

'*Oh, Bill!*' Sue thought, and sprang.

It was a matter of a moment to strip off the baby's smoking rags.

'My bag! Quick!' she told the sobbing woman, who fled into the bedroom and rushed back with the bag.

The baby's body was burned, but only superficially, for its clothing had stopped the coals.

'That tea – on the chair!' Sue ordered.

'*Tea?*' The woman looked at Sue, stupefied.

'Yes! Hurry!'

Sue tore great handfuls of absorbent cotton from the roll she always carried, soaked them in the cold tea, and plastered them, brown and dripping, on the small body. The baby's screams rose higher with the shock of the cold and the mother's grimy hands came out to snatch her child from this strange woman. Sue's eyes stopped her, and in another moment the baby's screams were diminishing – to howls – to whimpers – to silence.

Sue wrapped it tenderly in her coat and turned to the woman.

'There!' she said gently. 'He'll – oh! *Your poor hands!*'

'My – land!' Mrs. Leffert whispered presently. 'Why – why, it – stopped th' hurt – almost right off – *plain tea!*'

'It'll do more than that,' Sue told her. 'There won't even be blisters, or any scar. But you must keep the cotton wet all the time for at least twenty-four hours. Don't let it dry out, especially on the baby. I don't believe you'll have to keep your hands bandaged overnight. You were so quick your burns weren't deep. Of course, with deep burns, cold tea alone isn't strong enough, but with surface burns it's fine.'

'I– I dunno how to thank you, nurse.'

'Don't,' said Sue comfortably. 'But you might tell me how all that happened.'

'Why – I was a pokin' up the fire a mite – had th' grate wide open. I guess th' stove was kinder full – an' I never see Jackie crawlin' up alongside of me. A whole great big mess of coals come pilin' out. They – they would have fallen on the floor – only – Jackie happened to – to be –'

'I see. Hadn't you better go and tell Mr. Leffert that everything's all right now? He must be scared stiff. Oh, and you really ought to keep a jar of cold tea on hand all the time. It's very handy for small burns when you're cooking.'

'I'ma goin' to, I can tell ye!'

The outside door opened suddenly and Bill's tall figure filled the smoky room.

'What – ' he began.

Sue explained, and he nodded, his eyes warm on her face. 'Good girl,' he said. 'I've got a tube of tannic acid that will finish the job.'

They drove away at last, up the winding, snowy road, followed by Mrs. Leffert's almost garrulous good-byes. The fresh mountain wind blew cold in their faces, and the sky arched above them, infinitely blue.

'Honey,' Bill said abruptly, 'you're a darling!'

'Thank you, Doctor. And now what?'

'Nothing – except lunch.'

'I meant after lunch.'

'Nothing – for you. I have patients to attend to, but you aren't supposed to be my surgery nurse.'

'Aren't you going to make any visits this afternoon?'

'Nope.'

'You mean I'm through for the day?'

'Why, yes,' Bill said lightly – too lightly. 'You wouldn't be, if you were all established and had your own car, but –'

'Couldn't I be getting acquainted with a lot of your patients if I helped you in the surgery? After all, I *haven't* got my car yet, and –'

'There really isn't anything for you to do – unless I get an outside call. If I do I'll let you know. How'd you like to go to a church supper with me tonight?'

'Love to! But –'

'That's fine,' he said quickly. 'Lord, Sue! This accident at the Lefferts' is going to do more to put you in solid at Harville than three months of ordinary work would do. The way you used the tea will be all over the place inside of fifteen minutes, and it's just the kind of thing to appeal to the people as a definite proof of genius. It's not that I don't sympathize with the Lefferts, God knows – only the thing *was* a lucky break for you!'

'I know. But it's going to be an awfully slow business; I can see that.'

'Well, if even one family improves in the course of a year it'll be a bigger step forward than you have any idea of at present. Lord! What a hill!' He turned his attention to the car and nothing more was said about Sue's coming to the surgery.

10

Typhoid

SUE was to remember the next two weeks as a nightmare which bore no relation to the passage of time. Everything seemed to have happened at once, although, in reality, there were ten comparatively quiet days between Bill's confession and the beginning of the typhoid epidemic. The arrival of Marianna and her own new car were just dim events in the miserable confusion.

It all began with the church supper, which had been like any other church supper in any small New England town. Lights glared down from the town-hall ceiling on long tables set with thick white dishes and loaded with food. There were plates of fried chicken, pots of baked beans, home-made brown-flaked pies, mountainous layer-cakes, sugared doughnuts, green jars of pickles, the clear crimson and amber of jellies, the pale ivory of sweet butter.

There was the familiar confusion and noise: small boys slid across the floor and clambered over benches; men's heavy boots clumped; stout matrons in kitchen aprons hurried back and forth; little girls giggled. High-school boys showed off and high-school girls pretended not to see them. Men gravitated together in low-pitched solemn groups as soon as they had eaten, while their wives bustled capably.

Sue and Bill arrived early and were served with such despatch that in less than half an hour they had finished and there seemed nothing to do but go home. They lingered for a time, however, talking with friends and acquaintances. Sue recognized several members of the Farm Club and stopped to speak with them. Lot Phinney was there accompanied by a quiet and amiable Mrs. Phinney. Ira Prouty grinned at Sue across the tables. But Sue's acquaintances in Springdale were few as yet and she was ready to leave before Bill had made his own personal round of the hall.

The main room was hot and Sue stepped out into the entry for a breath of fresh air. A murmur of male voices came from outside, on the front steps.

'They say,' she heard, 'that he dunno beans when th' bag's open. Admits it himself, too. Says he dunno where that typhoid's a comin' frum. Always thought he was a likely young feller m'self, but seems as though a doctor that knowed his job would of found out about that typhoid long ago.'

A cold sick feeling clutched at the pit of Sue's stomach and prickled her scalp.

'That's so,' came a second voice. 'Take a thing like that to show a body up. Guess likely he's all right for cuts an' pimples, but no doctor at all's better'n a bum one. Feller like that's a danger to th' community.'

'There's a lot beginnin' to feel that way. They say –'

Sue didn't wait to hear any more, but turned and fled back into the hall. Bill was still talking – to Mrs. Tom Ventress, the town's fat woman, without whose famous ice-cream no church supper was complete. Bill's dark head was bent in interested and friendly attention. He didn't look up.

Sue wanted to scream.

The wait, however, gave her time to collect her thoughts. She mustn't upset Bill with an account of what she had heard until she had had a chance to talk with Veazie Ann – calm, sensible Veazie Ann! But she must get him out of here! She must find out if he had any inkling of what was going on.

He glanced up at last and Sue caught his eye. He nodded and, excusing himself as quickly as he could, joined her.

'You look all in,' he said. 'Want to go home?'

It wasn't until they were well out on the valley road that Sue asked quietly, 'Bill – why didn't you want me to come to the surgery this afternoon? I know you didn't, and it's been worrying me. Is anything wrong?'

Bill hesitated a second too long. 'Why – why, no. Of course not.'

There was a little silence. The road spun backwards beneath them, white in the glare of the headlights, and the valley dropped away, a trough of darkness in the shadow of the mountains.

'There *is* something, Bill,' said Sue at last. 'You might as well tell me.'

The dim light from the instrument panel enclosed them in a tiny swaying room in which only their faces were distinct – Sue's pale and intent, Bill's expressionless at first, then suddenly resolved.

'All right,' he said, 'perhaps I'd better. I – Sue, my practice is falling off – a lot. I didn't tell you because I didn't want to worry you. And besides, I wasn't sure – in the beginning. I thought it might be chance – or a dull spell.'

'But it isn't?'

'No,' Bill said slowly, 'it isn't.'

'Have you any idea why?'

He shook his head. 'That's the devil of it. I haven't the faintest idea.' He stared at the oncoming road and the middle finger of his left hand went to his moustache in the familiar, puzzled gesture.

Sue tried to be matter-of-fact and calm. 'When did you begin to notice it?' she asked.

Bill grinned rather feebly. 'When my patients began to get fewer.'

'When was that?'

'A month or two ago.'

'About the time you started chasing down the typhoid?'

He glanced at her quickly. 'What's on your mind, sweet?'

Sue shrugged. 'Oh, nothing special. I just thought you might have mentioned around that you didn't understand it.'

'Well, I did. Why shouldn't I?'

Sue reached out to lay an apologetic hand on his arm. 'Look, darling,' she said, 'I don't want to go sticking a whole boatful of oars into your business – but I remember that Dad used to say that only about one person in a hundred thought better of a doctor for saying he didn't know something. He said people always expected a doctor to be superhuman, and that if he admitted, right out loud, that he was stuck, it scared them half to death.'

Bill gave a faint, startled whistle.

'Good Lord!' he said. Then, 'But hold on! That's all very well – as far as it goes – but it doesn't go far enough. The people round here are pretty level-headed. I don't believe my saying now and then that I couldn't seem to trace the source of infection would set them all by the ears this way. It isn't reasonable. I think there's something else behind it.'

'You mean' – Veazie Ann's words came back to Sue – 'that somebody has a spite against you, and is spreading things about you?'

'Something like that,' Bill admitted.

'What makes you think so?'

He told her, then, all that she already knew of the attacks upon him. 'And if,' he finished, 'it doesn't stop pretty soon, I'm going to be a fine upstanding young doctor who would like a permanent position as a grocer's clerk.'

'Oh, *no*, Bill! Is it really as bad as that?'

'I'm afraid it is. But I'm going to be a noble hero and stick it out, no matter what.'

Sue's fingers tightened on his arm. 'I'll stick along with you. We can start a Co-ed Scout movement and be all the members.'

Sue's tone was not so light, however, when she told Veazie Ann what had happened.

Veazie Ann rarely went to church suppers and Sue found her getting ready for bed – a stout, comfortable figure in a long-sleeved, high-necked flannel nightgown. It billowed balloon-like around her as she stood before the mirror, patiently putting her hair up in curlers.

'It's cold enough in here to break your breath off,' she said.

'You go and poke up the fire in the kitchen while I git me into a wrapper.'

And so, while they toasted their feet in the kitchen oven, Sue unburdened herself.

'I wouldn't git too haired up,' Veazie Ann said, her curlers quivering with every move of her head. 'Folks'll always talk. If everybody was a feelin' that way about the doctor I'd of heard it.'

'You might not. You've been at home a good deal lately. Veazie Ann – what ought I to do? Should I tell him?'

'Least said's soonest mended. I shouldn't. There's no call to upset him on account of a lot of loose talk. You wait a while – and keep your ears open. Meantime, I'll stir round a mite; mebbe I can find out sumpthin'.'

But neither of them learned anything new. Their closeness to Bill was an effective silencer. Veazie Ann, after a week of assiduous calling on friends, admitted that she was stumped. 'All I can git,' she said, 'is a kind of a look. Some have it and some don't. But seems to me things ain't as bad as the doctor thinks. It's my notion, if he'll keep right on a goin', 's if nothin' was happenin', the hull thing'll blow over. Folks git dretful crazy ideas, and make such a to-do agin somebody ye'd think they was all special lions a gittin' ready fer Daniel. Works out just about the same way, too. If ye set right there and pay no attention, after a while it comes to 'em mebbe this ain't the meal they thought 'twas. It's kinder miserable awaitin'; but the minute one of 'em quits a lickin' of his chops and starts sayin' *he* was only foolin' – the hull kit 'n' billin'll start to purr.'

'You're sweet, Veazie Ann,' said Sue, trying to feel encouraged. She was sleeping badly most of the time now, and it seemed to her she did nothing these days except watch faces which told her nothing. She went about her work automatically, scarcely conscious of it, but she must have done it as well as usual, for more and more smiles greeted her as she made her rounds – on foot and in Springdale at first, then, when her car came, to outlying farms and villages. She did dressings; she bathed new babies; she combined roller skates and a rocking chair to make a wheel chair; she gave treatments; she kept up her records – all in a daze.

The Red Cross car was a comfortable sedan, and as people learned of its arrival more and more calls came over Veazie Ann's telephone. Sue responded faithfully, but she was loyal to her Henry Street training and would not make more than three visits to any family without a doctor's supervision – and the only doctor was Bill. Sometimes he was called, and sometimes Sue's third visit to a house was her last.

She wondered what her sponsors in the Farm Club thought of all this and finally asked Mrs. Edgett.

'They got nothin' agin you,' said that lady crisply. 'You're doin' fine. As fer th' doctor, they got more minds'n a hen crossin' th' road, an' they can't do nothin' about it. When it comes to your connection with him – wimmin generally feel fer a girl when her man's in trouble – no matter what they think about him.'

'But what *do* they think about him?'

'They don't say nothin' to me about it – they know better! All I git's distant rumblin's. Land, I wisht th' doctor had his hospital he wants so much! I says to 'em t'other day, I says, "Ye'd be better a raisin' him th' money for a hospital than a runnin' him down," I says. "*I'll* give a passel of my land for't, any time," I says. But o' course, there ain't nothin' they can really do.'

Sue was touched by this loyalty, though she couldn't help feeling that discretion on Mrs. Edgett's part would be more helpful than so much valour. Still – her influence would help stem the tide that was turning against Bill. Sue went on her way vaguely hopeful.

Her skis and snowshoes were sent on from home, and with them came a raccoon coat – a present from her father. Sue was delighted, naturally, but her worry about Bill overshadowed everything else. Even Marianna's arrival, which ordinarily would have been a great event, now seemed unimportant.

Marianna came towards the end of those ten quiet days – a wildly excited Marianna, thrilled at being with Sue, astonished by the country and, oddly enough, a little frightened by it. Marianna could sleep in doorways and roam the city streets at night without a qualm, but here, in the unfamiliar country, she was afraid.

The mountains overwhelmed her and she stared at them in awed silence. Springdale she regarded with amazement. 'You mean that's the *town*? Why, there ain't nothin' there but houses! Is that where I'm going to school?'

'Why not?' said Sue. 'It's a very good school.'

Marianna's devotion to Sue prevented her from expressing herself freely. Although she was nineteen and in her second year at high school, she was slow to respond to people. Her quick eyes swept over Veazie Ann's homely, comfortable rooms with growing bewilderment. Everything astonished her – the wood box, the oil lamps, the stove in the front room, the wing chairs, the feather beds, the zinc tub in the bathroom to which water must be carried in pails.

Sue had worried, at first, about Marianna and Veazie Ann, but she need not have done so. Marianna was a little dazed by Veazie Ann's house dresses and by her speech, but Marianna, despite her ignorance, was no fool. She knew personality when she saw it, and five minutes with Veazie Ann reduced Marianna to a state of profound respect. As for Veazie Ann – she had been prepared by Sue for Marianna's peculiarities, and her attitude from the first was one of kindly indulgence.

'What's that?' Marianna asked her, looking out of the window.

'It's a well, child.'

'What's a well?'

'Suz alive!' Veazie Ann exclaimed involuntarily. Then, 'It's where we get our water.'

Marianna stared at her, round-eyed. 'Ya – ya mean,' she faltered, 'ya gotta drink water outa th' *ground*?'

Sue took a hand at this point. 'And where, my lamb, do you think New York gets its water?'

'From pipes!'

'Surely – but the pipes draw it from lakes – which are in the ground too.'

'Gee!' Marianna said slowly. 'I guess I never thought about that before.'

At nightfall she became really terrified. The hooting of an owl, followed by the ringing boom of ice cracking across a near-by pond, brought her out of her chair with a leap. Wild-eyed, she heard the pistol-like report of twigs snapping in the cold, and the splintering crash of a falling icicle. Once she insisted that there was someone on the roof, and Sue, listening, recognized the yattering sound made by a broken branch sliding on crusted snow.

'G-olly!' Marianna quavered, when Sue had explained. 'I – I s-pose you get used to it?'

'Of course! Inside of a week you won't even notice.' Sue hesitated a moment. Then she added, 'If I were you I wouldn't ask too many questions of the kids at school – about country things, I mean.'

Marianna nodded. 'I get it. It would be same as if one of them come to N'York. They'd get laughed at, I guess. When am I gonna start?'

'I've made arrangements for you to begin on Monday. I thought you'd better have a few days to get used to things. You'll start as a second-year student, and if you do as well as you did at night school they'll probably move you into the junior class. Meantime you can go around with me in the car.'

'Swell!'

But by Monday seven cases of typhoid had broken out – four in the village, three on farms outside. Within a week there were twelve more!

The village was in an uproar. Sue, answering calls, found again and again the familiar symptoms, heard repeatedly the same history of backache, headache, loss of appetite, sore muscles, sore throat, nosebleeds, and at last fever – 104 and 105 degrees – with flushed faces, hot dry skins, bloodshot eyes. Each time, while the story was being repeated, Sue examined the patient's chest and abdomen, and each time she found the dreaded rose spots – tiny raised spots that disappeared for almost a minute after being pressed with the finger. Then Sue called Bill, who was nearly always received by the family with sullen resentment.

'You'd better,' he told Sue unhappily, 'carry a batch of sterile test tubes with you. There's no reason why you shouldn't take a blood specimen; I'd have to do the Widal test here at the surgery, anyway.'

This cleared the atmosphere a little, but Sue very quickly ceased to hope that any of the blood tests would prove negative. At first she hung over Bill's shoulder, watching breathlessly while he did the Widal test. It was a very simple test. Bill combined a drop of the patient's blood serum with a culture of typhoid bacilli obtained from the State Board of Health, put the mixture under the microscope, and watched grimly. Each time the vigorous, swimming bacilli stopped moving and clumped together. Each time, Bill said with growing despair, '*Positive Widal!*'

Questioning of the patients revealed a very confusing series of facts. Every individual who had been taken ill had been at the church supper – but not everyone who was there was ill. And those infected had eaten a great variety of things. There was only one thing which everybody had eaten – Mrs. Ventress's famous ice cream; yet, of the fifty or more persons who had attended the supper and eaten the ice cream, only eighteen had gone down with typhoid. The big freezer, of course, had long since been washed and put away, and while a typhoid bacillus can live for some time outside the human body if given plenty of moisture, it could not possibly survive two weeks in a dry, metal freezer. Nor could it live so long on dry dishes. Mrs. Ventress had a Widal test at once. It was negative. The milk was the next thing – and it had come from the local dairy, which had been tested thoroughly at the time of the first outbreak of typhoid. Bill, however, went out to the dairy and went through the whole thing again – the only result being to infuriate the owner of the dairy.

Sue and Bill worked frantically, trying to inoculate the entire village and near-by farm population with anti-typhoid vaccine.

Bill's surgery was crowded the first day. Then the numbers began to dwindle. Sue dashed from house to house, trying to persuade, to explain.

' 'Tain't no use, Miss Barton,' the people told her. 'We ain't got nothin' against you – but we ain't a goin' to let *him* give us *all* typhoid!'

'What on earth do you mean?' Sue cried. 'He's trying to keep you from having it! I know everybody is frightened, but surely you understand about vaccines?'

'Not with him a givin' 'em, we don't.'

'But *why*?'

They looked at her pityingly and shrugged.

The arrival of old Dr. Vinal, the Board of Health officer from Winslow, saved the day. He was a gentle, understanding old man, well known in the community, and in the end it was he who gave the inoculations, assisted by Sue.

'It'll blow over,' he told the haggard Bill. 'Even sensible folks will get in a panic once in a while, and act unreasonable. Keep your chin up, boy!'

The Winslow Hospital took ten of the cases – all it had beds for – and Dr. Vinal, at Bill's request, agreed to send a young assistant to see those ill at home.

'I'll do what I can to talk 'em out of this nonsense,' he said, 'but I doubt if it'll do much good just now. Maybe I can persuade 'em to let you treat 'em by telephone – you've got a nurse to take your orders. Too bad you don't have a hospital here.'

'It would be empty, if I had,' Bill said grimly.

'Now, now! Don't let it get you down. You've still got friends here. The first selectman swears by you, and I've heard that Prouty feller giving people what-for down at the Eat-a-While. And all your patients haven't turned you down.'

This was true. A few of Bill's old patients were loyal to him, and Harville was solidly behind him. There was no typhoid in Harville, but had there been it would have made no difference. Bill was their own doctor and that was that.

Dr. Vinal, before he left, did persuade a good many of the typhoids to allow Bill to treat them by telephone. They had faith in Sue at any rate. But a young Dr. Howard was sent by the Board of Health nonetheless, for someone must test the water-supplies, and the people would not allow Bill near their wells. It was this last obstinacy which revealed the new terror which had taken root in people's minds.

'We don't want no typhoid carriers around our well,' they said.

So that was it – they believed Bill to be a typhoid carrier.

'But what gave them such a notion?' Sue wailed. 'What do they know about carriers?'

'I told you!' Bill said. 'Somebody is deliberately starting these things. But who? Why?'

'Do you remember,' said Sue slowly, 'that the famous Typhoid Mary believed that she was the victim of a persecution by doctors, and that they went around giving people typhoid to make money for themselves – and deliberately put the blame on her?'

'I know. It – it could be, Sue. But who is it and where are -- is he – she – it?'

That question remained unanswered in spite of all Bill's efforts. But the newspapers around the state, perceiving that here was an exciting story, played up the townspeople's belief that Bill was a typhoid carrier. This made matters so much worse that by the time a statement was published by Dr. Vinal, saying that Dr. Barry had had a Widal test and was proved free of typhoid, no one believed it.

'Doctors'll stick together!' one man told the outraged Veazie Ann.

The state sent a Visiting Nurse to help Sue. Mrs. Barton wrote frantically to ask what was going on. And Sue longed for Kit.

'She'd keep all our spirits up,' Sue thought, remembering the happy days when she and Kit and Connie had worked together in the hospital – when Bill had been a carefree young interne, marked for a brilliant future. Kit had been an expert typhoid nurse, even in her students days. 'And, so of course, she has to be in New York,' said Sue bitterly to Marianna.

All told, twenty-five cases of typhoid appeared, in and around Springdale – inclusive of the first. But when two weeks passed without a new case the village began to grow calmer, and the State Nurse returned to her work in another county.

'All the same,' Bill remarked one night, 'I'm afraid I'm done for in Springdale, darling. There was a chance until they got this crazy idea that I'm the carrier. Even then, if the newspapers had kept out of it – but as it is, no matter where I might go from here, people would be afraid of me. I might get a good start somewhere else, but if a single case of typhoid appeared this story would be raked up.'

'Then – w-what can you do?' Sue faltered.

'My standing in the profession is just as good as ever. I could go into lab. work, and do research. Research has never appealed to me much, but I suppose I'd get to like it.'

He tried to speak cheerfully, but his voice was heavy.

They were sitting, as they had sat so many times, in Veazie Ann's front room, Sue curled in the arm-chair, with Bill at her feet. Her face was colourless with fatigue and Bill's was drawn and hollow-eyed.

'You ought to be in bed,' he said, looking at her weary young face in sudden compunction. 'I'll go home.'

'No, don't go yet. I'm not as tired as all that. Bill, if the carrier were found you'd be all right, wouldn't you?'

'I might. It would be a lot better if I could find the carrier myself instead of having him turn up by accident – which may very well happen. But I'm not able to work on that angle any more. People will hardly let me pass them on the street without sheering off as if I had the plague. I can't get near any of the people I need to see about it.' He hesitated. Then he said, 'There's another thing – I can't stick on much longer because of Eliot. I've got to have money for him very soon. I can borrow if I have to – but I'm hoping something will happen. Young Howard may find something in some water-supply.'

'How – how long can you hold out without getting into debt?'

'About another month. At least, for myself. I've sent Eliot nearly all I have. He'd be all right for several months. But I still have to eat, and I'm helpless here because of the feeling about me. I can't do a thing.'

'I might,' said Sue quietly.

'What do you mean?'

'I get around a lot these days. I could ask questions. I might dig up some clue. If I did, I could just say nothing and pass it on to you, and –'

'Oh no, you don't! Go ahead and ask questions. Maybe you *will* find something – but if you do, you take the credit. Is that clear?'

'Very.'

'Okay. Then I'm going home and let you go to bed.' He scrambled to his feet, bent over to kiss her, and was gone.

Sue, however, did not go to bed after he left. She sat for a long time beside the old stove in the front room – thinking harder, it seemed to her, than she had ever thought in all her life before.

11

Sue Barton - detective

SUE'S plans, however, had to be carried out when she could find the extra time. Pressure of work during the epidemic was giving her little chance to make other visits. The typhoids who had not gone to the hospital were scattered over the village and out in the hills. Sue was the only nurse constantly available, and while it was not difficult to teach some member of each family how to give bed-baths and alcohol sponges, and how to swab dry mouths and prevent bedsores, there remained the always present possibility of intestinal perforation – and Sue could not be everywhere at once.

She would have liked to make two visits a day to each patient, but this was impossible. A great deal of time was taken up in giving cold packs – a lengthy process, in which the miserable patient must be wrapped in icy wet sheets to reduce his temperature. She had to watch diets and be ready with instructions on how to make whey, koumiss, and an endless variety of gruels, and all that she could do, in place of a second visit, was to impress on the patients' families the necessity of reporting immediately any attack of nausea, the slightest sign of hiccoughs, and, above all else, a sudden sharp pain.

'There would only be one and it would be sharp,' she repeated patiently. 'Remember now – just one *sharp* pain! Call Dr. Barry's surgery at once!' She added a little grimly, 'If you won't have Dr. Barry, he'll get in touch with somebody else.' She hated to alarm the families. Perforations seldom occurred nowadays, and some abdominal pain is not at all unusual in typhoid – but there was no other way to keep everyone in the house on the alert. Long days and nights of nursing, when nothing happened, were likely to put amateur nurses off their guard, and while the pain which accompanies perforation is different from ordinary cramps, its briefness might cause it to be overlooked.

Sue's car was on the road from early morning until long after dark, in spite of the fact that the days were lengthening notice-ably now that March had come. She did her best to answer emer-gency calls as well. A small boy, injured tobogganing, delayed her so long one day that she didn't reach the homes of the last three typhoids on her list until well into the evening. The child's family refused to have Bill called on the case, and Sue didn't dare leave until the Red Cross doctor – still testing water-supplies – could be located. A farmer living alone was dis-covered unconscious on the barn floor by a neighbour, who, since the patient was 'no relative of hisn', called Bill. The man was seriously ill with pneumonia, and another case was added to Sue's list, though Bill did what he could to help her here.

Sue took Marianna with her when she could – which was seldom. She was seeing very little of Marianna now, for by nightfall Sue was too tired to sit up talking. She realized that all this was hard on a city-bred youngster, who was accustomed to noise and excitement, but it couldn't be helped. Sue wished, sometimes, that she had not urged Marianna to come to Spring-dale at just this time. A month or two later would have been much better.

Marianna, however, made no complaint, said she thought she was doing all right at school, and offered no further com-ment. She was, in fact, unusually silent around the house. Sue was vaguely aware of this, but had no energy to spare for enter-tainment. Marianna would have to bear up as best she could for a while.

Meantime Sue was skipping her lunch daily in order to pursue her quiet investigations. She knew that time and patience would be required to unravel the tangle of events, but she was certain it could be done. The drives from one patient to another gave her a chance to think back over all that had happened, and it seemed to her that a pattern was beginning to emerge from what had, at first, appeared to be coincidence.

There were the mysterious attacks on Bill, which had begun

about the time the first two cases of typhoid had appeared. Why should they have begun just then? The word 'Quack' had been scratched on Bill's car as it stood outside the home of those first two cases. Whoever had done that had been trying, very clumsily, to discredit him – a sure sign that somebody was afraid of him. Bill's headlamps had been smashed immediately following the second outbreak of typhoid – a senseless and vindictive act of no great importance in itself, but nonetheless a straw which showed the direction of the wind, for it had been Bill who had diagnozed the cases as *typhoid*. And now here was this frenzied attempt to label Bill as the carrier.

Whoever was doing all this *must* be a man, Sue thought. Women are less prone to physical violence. Furthermore, a woman would be unlikely to go prowling around the countryside at night picking a car as an object of revenge. But whoever he was, he was not wholly stupid – else how had he managed to remain undiscovered? Every known person in the village had been examined for typhoid and all except the patients themselves had been found negative. So the carrier must live outside the town, and wherever he lived his drains must be full of typhoid bacilli. He couldn't even throw out a dishpanful of water without the bacilli seeping down into a near-by spring or brook. Yet both Bill and the Red Cross doctor had examined all the drains, wells, springs, and brooks for miles around – and had found nothing.

The man couldn't be a stranger or he would have been noticed. He couldn't be a passing tramp or he would have been gone long before he had time to do so much damage. He had obviously been at the church supper. But how on earth had he infected grandmother and child, or the men shovelling snow?

The only thing to do was to look for a stupid, ignorant man, known to everybody. 'And,' Sue thought, 'I'd better start at the very beginning, with the Masons – grandmother and child.'

So, one noon, she drove to the little white house carrying some ice cream, and while her patients ate it with the avid hunger of all convalescing typhoids, Sue led the conversation round to the days preceding their illness.

'I know,' she told old Mrs. Mason, 'that everybody has been asking you questions about this, but I thought perhaps – now you're so much better – your memory might be clearer. You wouldn't, maybe, recall your son's having had somebody here for dinner about that time?'

'No, he didn't, Miss Barton. I'm real sure about that. We ain't much for entertainin' folks.'

'And he didn't hire anybody to work round the place for a day – somebody who had his noon meal in the house, or came in for a drink of water?'

'No, he never. George ain't had much work this winter, and whatever's been done around the place, he done himself.'

'I see.' There was nothing to be learned from Mrs. Mason. Sue tried the little girl with no better results. Frances ate lunch at school, but it was always prepared at home. She hadn't eaten anything from any other child's lunch as nearly as she could remember. She hadn't brought anything home to Grannie from anywhere. In fact, the only food they had shared, which had not been shared by the rest of the family, had been the daily quart of milk – which got Sue exactly nowhere, for the dairy's milk had been tested and the drivers were healthy young men without a single typhoid bacillus among them. Still, it would do no harm to inquire there.

Sue drove out to the dairy farm next day, through a snow-storm – for March brings few signs of spring in the mountains. The sky is a little softer, perhaps, but ice and snow remain and blizzards still sweep across the ranges.

The farmer who owned the dairy received Sue with repressed fury.

'No,' he said. 'I don't know nothin' about this typhoid business, an' there's been enough talk goin' around about my milk!'

'But Mr. Taggart, don't you see – if we could find out who the carrier is – that would clear you, definitely.'

'I got a pretty good idea who 'tis!'

Sue swallowed her rising anger. 'It isn't Dr. Barry,' she said. *'Really* it isn't! He's been tested. I think it's somebody who lives in the country and goes into town a lot. If you could help me just a little –'

'Well, I can't. 'Tain't nobody here!'

'But –'

'I said 'tain't!'

Sue gave up the struggle and went back to her car. She could still interview the man's drivers – if she could catch them in town. There were two – one living at the dairy farm, the other in Springdale. The first brought Veazie Ann's milk, and Sue rose wearily at dawn the next morning to waylay him. He was willing to be helpful but he knew nothing of any value. The boss hadn't hired any new men in a year. No, he didn't deliver to the Masons. Jimmy Bowker done that.

Sue found Jimmy Bowker at home that evening. He was just a lad, living with his parents, a pleasant boy, shyly pleased at being interviewed by the town's pretty new nurse.

'No, ma'am,' he said awkwardly. 'I'm afraid I can't help ye none. There ain't nobody handles the milk but us drivers and the fellers that run th' milkin' machines. We all been on the job a long time.'

'But you do deliver to the Masons, don't you?'

'Yes'm, I do. Gosh! I guess I ain't likely to ferget it, neither.'

'Does Mr. Taggart buy any milk from other farmers?'

'Not very often – sometimes, in th' spring, along in April or May.'

'Would you know it if you delivered any milk to the Masons that didn't come from the Taggart farm?'

'I dunno's I would. It's already bottled when we take it – but anyhow, the boss warn't buyin any milk from anybody in January and February.'

'And nobody's been hired, even for a day?'

'Not't I know of.'

'You don't ever have any helpers on the milk route?'

'No, ma'am.'

The next on Sue's list was Ira Prouty. He and the lorry driver were the only ones in the snow-shovelling gang who had not had typhoid. The remaining three men were all in Winslow Hospital and she had no time to go there.

Ira was working at Bald Trail Inn, helping round the grounds, and Sue drove out the following day. She found him in the tool shed, eating his lunch in the company of the carpenter who had directed Sue to the kennels the day she came to see Elias Todd.

She didn't want to discuss the matter of the typhoids before the carpenter. The less public her efforts the better.

The men were sitting in the toolhouse doorway and looked up amiably as Sue's red head appeared over a rise of ground.

'Good morning,' she said briskly. 'I'm so sorry to disturb you, Ira, but that funny little gadget you fixed on my car the other day doesn't seem to be working. Could you spare half a minute to look at it?'

Ira's mouth opened slightly and he stared at her in blank bewilderment.

Sue returned his stare with such compelling urgency that his mouth closed. 'Oh – er – sure,' he said, rising.

As soon as they were out of earshot of the carpenter Sue explained, and while the grinning Ira fumbled under the hood of Sue's car for the imaginary gadget, she leaned on the fender, talking.

'Did that road gang always have the same men in it, Ira?'

'Well, no. Did most of the time. But now'n agin somebody laid off for sumpthin' an' the boss hired somebody else. So you might say the men was kinder comin' and goin'.'

'It *would* have to be like that! Did you all eat lunch together?'

'Ayah – guess we did,' said Ira from the insides of the car. 'Jiminy, Miss Barton, it's real kinder comfortable round this engine. Glad you brung me out. I kin get my hands warm!'

Sue laughed, and Ira went on. 'The doctor ast me that, too.

Wanted to know 'f we swapped vittles or drunk outer the same bucket.'

'Did you?'

'Yup, just about all the time – and that makes it kinder tough for you, don't it?' His voice was gruffly sympathetic. 'Want ye to know,' he said with suddenly pink ears, 'that I don't take no stock in all that truck about th' doctor.'

'Thank you, Ira,' said Sue. 'You've been a good friend to both of us. And we – we need friends just now.'

'You got plenty, Miss Barton, and so's th' doctor. It's just that folks has kinder lost their heads right now. They'll git over it in a little spell. And anyway, they ain't got nothin' agin you, as 'tis.'

'I know. But you see, in the meantime Dr. Barry isn't making even a living. He can't go on like that for ever.'

Ira withdrew his head from under the hood and straightened up. 'I never thought of that, 'he said slowly. 'It's too darned bad! I'd – be real glad to help you and him if I can.'

'I'm afraid there isn't much you could do, Ira, except to try to remember something that would give us a clue to the carrier. Isn't there *anything* that happened or anybody who, maybe, worked with you for a day and drank from your water bucket, or gave you some of his coffee?'

Ira pushed his worn felt hat to the back of his head and stood motionless, struggling to remember.

'I can't think of nobody special,' he said. 'I'm awful sorry, Miss Barton. There was quite a few worked a couple of days at a time, but they've all had their tests. And ye can't remember little things, goin' so fur back, without somethin' comes up to remind ye.'

'No, I suppose you can't. And none of it makes a bit of sense.' She smiled at him suddenly. 'Maybe that's the trouble. Maybe we shouldn't try to be so reasonable.' Sue's eyes began to twinkle. 'Probably what we ought to do,' she said, 'is look for somebody who's been secretly courting Grandma Mason in the guise of a travelling salesman. That might lead us to discover that one day about a month ago a man who seemed to be Lot Phinney came and asked your foreman to please, please, give him just an hour's work, shovelling snow with you boys, because he was dying of hunger and thirst, and –'

'Like enough,' said Ira gravely. 'An' then we'd find that he went to the church supper, all dressed up to look like Mrs. Tom Ventress, an' served everybody ice cream.' His gravity broke as Sue's laughter rang out at the thought of anybody trying to look like the 20-stone Mrs. Ventress.

Sue was still laughing when she drove away. Ira Prouty was always fun. But even he, she thought, soberly, couldn't seem to help her in this case, however willing he might be.

'I'll just have to plod along without help,' she told herself, 'and do the best I can. I guess Mrs. Ventress is next.'

12

Clue?

Sue's call on Mrs. Ventress was made on a Saturday two days later and she stopped by the house to ask Marianna to go with her.

Veazie Ann heard the car and came out.

'I'm real glad,' she said, when Sue explained. 'If ye ain't too tired, Sue, I wish ye'd try to cheer her up a mite. They tell me the young ones at the high school ain't as friendly with her's they could be. Shouldn't wonder 'f she's a feelin' it. She's pretty glum around the house.'

Sue was startled and contrite. 'The poor lamb!' she exclaimed. 'Of course I will, Veazie Ann. Thanks for telling me. I'm afraid I haven't paid much attention to her lately.'

Cheering Marianna was uphill work. She answered Sue's questions about school in monosyllables, and though her manner was pleasant enough, the old sulkiness was in her eyes. Sue was really worried, but she had no chance to do anything about it then, for the rambling old Ventress house was already in sight at the end of the valley below the ancient dam which held back the waters of Springdale Lake. The lake was still frozen – a narrow, winding ice sheet – though a little open water was visible along the dam, and the thunder of its fall was already so near that Sue, trying to make conversation, had to raise her voice. Her choice of a topic had very unexpected results.

'There'd be plenty happening around here,' she remarked, looking up, 'if that dam ever broke. It was built in 1870 and –'

'It can bust any time it likes, for all of me,' Marianna said with such savage bitterness that Sue was shocked.

'Why, *Marianna*! What *is* it?'

Marianna took a deep breath. 'Nothin',' she said. Then,

quickly, 'Honest! I'm just kinder blue today. Ain't that the driveway to where you're goin'?'

Sue hastily turned her attention to the road and neither of the girls spoke again until the car rolled to a stop before the Ventress door.

'I'll wait here,' Marianna said. 'You g'wan in.'

Sue left her reluctantly, wishing that Marianna had picked some other time to be temperamental, since there was nothing that could be done about it at the moment. The gigantic billows that were Mrs. Tom Ventress already filled the open doorway, and Sue was rushed into the parlour to find herself seated before a cascade of double chins.

'Goodness!' she thought wildly. 'Where was I? Marianna and Mrs. Ventress, between 'em, have got me completely off the track! Come on, Susie! Get yourself together!'

Her approach to the vital question of the ice cream required no tact since Mrs. Ventress had long since been cleared of any blame for what had happened, and she was openly thrilled at being part of the excitement.

'I've kept wondering about that ice cream,' Sue explained, 'until I'm in a perfect tizzy of curiosity, and I knew you wouldn't mind if I came and talked to you about it.'

Mrs. Ventress beamed. Curiosity was something she thoroughly understood.

'It was the only thing at the church supper,' Sue went on, 'which was eaten by everyone who is ill. What puzzles me is that it was also eaten by a lot of people who *aren't* ill, and I said to myself that if anybody would have any ideas about it, it would be you, Mrs. Ventress, since you served it, and were there all the time.'

The double chins wobbled. ' 'Tis funny,' Mrs. Ventress agreed. 'There was Cal Littlefield and his wife – they both et it, an' Cal was took down an' his wife warn't. I remember on account of Cal kinder complimentin' me on my ice cream. 'S' he, "Lura, there can't nobody beat ye, when 't comes t' ice cream," s' he. "I could set right down," s' he, "an' eat my way through a mountain of it." An' s' I, "I guess you're a tryin' to work me for a second helpin', ain't you, Cal?" An' s' he, "That's what! But ye'll hev to make it fast," s' he. "It's twenty-five minutes past eight now," 's' he, "an' I still got chores to do at home." So I brung him another dish, an' he et it an' went along.'

'His wife didn't have a second dish?'

'No, she didn't. Mrs. Ventress's moon face clouded. 'I — I wisht I knew who done it — but they's one thing I'm sartin of — 'twarn't Dr. Barry, for all they say 'twas. Ye can't tell me a pleasant-spoken young feller like that is full of them little germs. Besides, he warn't nowheres near that freezer. 'Twas out on the back stoop, an' he never went there. I told 'em so, right out. I sez, s' I —'

Her voice rambled on, shaking her chins, but Sue wasn't listening. She was thinking of Cal Littlefield, who received a *second* helping of ice cream at about eight-thirty.

'Mrs. Ventress!' Sue interrupted the flow. 'Could you remember what time Mr. Littlefield and his wife had their first helping of ice cream?'

'So then — oh! Why, I dunno's I can, eggsactly. Musta been around eight or a little after. I was servin' pretty steady all th' time. The only way I c'n guess is because Cal, he always eats his first helpin' kinder slow, testin' it. An' he'd just finished when he says, s' he, "Lura, there can't nobody beat ye wh —" '

'Who else had ice cream after that?'

'Well, le's see, there was 'Lisha Pringle, an' the Downeys, and Bijah Crowley an' his two young ones, an' —' She went on with a list of names.

Sue concealed her mounting excitement, maintaining as placid an expression as she could. Every person mentioned as having been served ice cream *after* Cal Littlefield was now ill of typhoid. But if there were anything in this, Mrs. Ventress mustn't realize it — yet. She'd have it all over town within half an hour. Furthermore, *Bill* must be the one to make discoveries — not Sue. There was, however, one more question.

Sue rose to her feet and buttoned her coat.

'Well,' she said, smiling, 'you've been awfully nice to bother with all my questions – no, don't get up, Mrs. Ventress. I'm afraid the whole thing is an awful muddle.' She took a step towards the door, and then turned, 'I don't suppose,' she said lightly, 'that there was anybody from any of the farms around who might have been out on the back stoop between eight and eighty-thirty?'

'Land, Miss Barton! Everbody was a goin' and a comin'! I had a sight to do, keepin' young ones an' dogs away frum that freezer. I come out oncet just in time to ketch that big hound of Lot Phinney's a whiskerin' over it – an' the sack that covered it was a lyin' on th' step, tho' how th' critter made out to pull it off, I can't see, an' I sez, s' I, *"You thievin' critter!"* I told Lot of it, straight off, an' he come an' got th' dog.'

'Thank you so much,' said Sue hastily. 'I won't bother you any longer. You've been –'

'Oh, 'tain't no bother, Miss Barton. Glad to hev ye. Come any time. If ye like caraway cookies I'm a goin' to make some to-morrer, an' –'

'I'd *love* to have some!' said Sue, backing out of the door.

She climbed into the car, started her engine, and drove away in an absorbed silence which Marianna made no effort to break. The roar of the waterfall grew faint and died away.

'But have I really got something,' Sue wondered, 'or is it just another blind alley?'

What was the value of knowing that everybody who was served ice cream after eight-thirty had been taken ill with typhoid, while those served before were still hearty? The fact, by itself, proved nothing – until one knew what persons had been hanging around the back of the town hall at that time. And even then, Sue thought bitterly, they'd all be found to have had negative Widal tests.

Sue longed to discuss the matter with Bill, but she couldn't possibly do that, she knew. Anything which might lead to the discovery of the carrier must seem to everybody to have been unearthed by Bill; and Bill, himself, must never doubt that he had done it. Sue had not spoken to him again of her plans, or mentioned that she was acting on them, and Bill, desperately worried by his enforced idleness, had most certainly forgotten all about the proposed detective work.

Sue stopped at his surgery on the way back and found him sitting at his desk, writing.

'Sue!' he cried, dropping his pen and leaping to his feet. 'I was hoping you'd turn up! I've got news.' He seemed quite light-hearted and Sue had a throb of hope that he had found some definite clue to the carrier.

His news, however, had nothing to do with the carrier.

'I've just got back from Winslow,' he said, looking down at her with a positively 'maternal' expression. 'The assistant superintendent of nurses – whose job we wanted for Kit – is leaving in April!' I've spoken to the trustees about Kit – and she can have the job. Are you pleased? D'you think she'd come so soon?'

'Oh, Bill! How perfectly gorgeous! Of *course* I'm pleased!' She took off her hat and ran her fingers through her hair. 'There are times,' she remarked softly, 'when I have definite suspicions that you're an awfully good guy!'

'So you've found me out,' he said modestly. 'Well, I knew I couldn't keep it from you for ever. Will you have a chair, Miss Barton, or would you like to come back later when the crowd of patients has thinned out?' He waved a hand at the empty waiting-room.

Sue swallowed, and laughed. 'I'll come back later after the rush – unless you could be induced to have dinner at the house. Could you bear it?'

'I could try,' he said with alacrity.

'All right. I'll tell Veazie Ann. What were you doing when I came in? Writing to Kit?'

He nodded. 'The trustees are writing to her, of course, but I thought I'd add my little bit. Want to put in a line?'

'No! Got to run! Give her my love and tell her I'm thrilled to death. G'bye!'

'*Hey!* Not so fast, my sweet!' He caught her in his arms and kissed her swiftly. Sue rubbed her ear against his chin. Whatever happened they were still together, and they'd stay together, and they could always make out. So everything was really all right.

'I've *got* to go, darling,' she said. 'It must be after one. I've millions of things to do – and Marianna's waiting in the car in an awful state of gloom over something. I think she probably needs a hearty lunch.'

'Want me to run her up to the house?'

'No, never mind. I've got to go by there, anyway.'

On the way back to Veazie Ann's Sue told Marianna the good news about Kit.

'That's swell,' Marianna said. 'I'm awful glad, Sue.'

'So'm I! Now we'll all be together again – in a way – and except for Connie.'

'You've kinder missed Connie, ain't you?'

'Well, naturally. But one gets used to being away from people after a while. And I think as you get older you don't depend on them quite so much. You get to stand on your own feet more.'

'I guess you think that's a good way to be, don't you?'

'Surely. Don't you?'

'I dunno,' said Marianna slowly. 'I never thought about it before. Anyway, I ain't had much practice dependin' on anybody – except – maybe – you an' Kit – just a little. I guess I been on my own most always. I done pretty good at it, too.'

'Oh yes – certainly!' said Sue, remembering the tough, bedraggled Marianna who had broken into the little house in New York; who had done so well on her own that she was sleeping in doorways at night and washing dishes in a saloon by day.

Both girls fell silent after Sue's comment, Marianna staring grimly across the valley at the mountains. Sue watching the road and thinking of Connie; of Kit; of the church supper and its tragic aftermath; of Bill, struggling against terrific odds; of the invisibility of the typhoid carrier.

This last thought had only to stir faintly in Sue's mind for her to pounce upon it. She did so now, going back over every known step in the recent developments, and she had just arrived at Ira Prouty's part in them – or, rather, his surprising lack of part – when the car reached home.

Veazie Ann's greeting was an announcement which fitted in neatly with Sue's train of thought.

'Ira Prouty telephoned, Sue. He wants you should come right up there if you can. He says he can't git off, an' he's got sumpthin' important to tell ye.'

'Oh, all right,' said Sue absently. Then, '*What? Oh my gosh!* Good-bye, everybody! See you later!'

13

End of the trail

IRA PROUTY was kneeling on a patch of soggy ground on the south side of Bald Trail Inn. A paint bucket stood in a melting snowdrift beside him, while his swiftly moving brush transformed the cellar window-sash from dingy grey to gleaming white. Above him a ground-floor window, already painted, stood open about three inches and warm air from inside swam out and up in a quivering stream.

Light footsteps on the path behind him brought Ira to his feet, his grey eyes crinkling with pleasure in his wind-burned narrow face.

'Well, if 'tain't!' he said. 'H'a ye, Miss Barton? Looks like ye got my message.'

'Yes.' Sue was breathless from running up the slope. 'What's happened, Ira?'

Ira turned his head to glance through the partly open window. The office inside was unoccupied.

'Mebbe I got sump'n an' mebbe I ain't,' he said. 'But you told me if I thought of anything at all – an' I have.'

'*What?*'

'Remember when we was a talkin' the other day – an' you was kinder foolin' – an' you said we'd oughter look, mebbe, for somebody who'd been a courtin' Grandma Mason disguised to be a travellin' salesman – or somebody who wanted jest an' hour's work a shovellin' snow, on account of he was a dyin' of hunger an' thirst?'

Sue nodded. There was no use in hurrying Ira. Her coat was suddenly too warm and too heavy, and she threw it open impatiently.

'Well, 'twas a funny thing – after you went off sump'n kept a botherin' me. Seemed like what you'd said hitched on to

sump'n. But I couldn't think what 'twas. Th' darned thing kept
me awake a chewin' on me same's if I was a cud.' He paused,
maddeningly, to wipe his hands on a paint rag.

Sue stood motionless, holding her breath. '*And then?*' she
exploded at last.

'I'm a gettin' to it. Well, 'twas this mornin' it come to me –
all at once. 'Twas that hour business done it. I knew 'twas
sump'n to do with that. Ye know old Jud Wherity?'

'I'm not sure. Seems to me I've heard of him. He's kind of a
tramp, isn't he?'

'You said it. Lives in a little old shack made outer Standard
Oil tins, up on the mountain back of town. Come here about
three years ago. Works around th' village till he gits him a
dollar or two, an' then lays up with his beer till th' money's
gone.'

'Yes, but what –

'I'm a tellin' ye. That day you run over the shovel – 'twas
around four o'clock. We hadn't but an hour to go afore quittin'
time. My hand warn't feelin' so good an I was standin' around,
half-way in the notion to quit then, when along come old Jud.
An' he says what was the matter with my hand? I told him, an'
he says did I think the boss would give him thirty-five cents for
an hour's work shovellin'? So I says sure. An' that's what happened. He did work an hour, tho' I never stayed to watch him.
An' he always has a killin' thirst. Likely he drunk half the
water outer the bucket; an' old Jud, he don't bother with no
fancy tin dippers – he jest gits right in all over. He was a drink-
in' when I left.'

'Oh, Ira! Do you think it *could* be? No – because everybody's had the Widal test.'

'I'll bet old Jud ain't. He hates a doctor worse'n pizen. Wun't
have nothin' to do with 'em. Says they're all quacks. An' nobody'd think of him because he ain't never round hardly any.
And 'tain't likely any of 'em run on his shack when they was a
testin' water. It's like pullin' hen's teeth to find it in them
woods.'

'Why didn't your truck driver get typhoid, do you suppose?'

'Likely he warn't thirsty – a settin' in that cold cab.'

'But the church supper – and the Masons.'

'I can't make no sense to the Masons – but he was at the church supper. He always goes an' hangs around the back for a handout an' a dish of ice cream. I see him on the way that night, a pokin' along like a old scarecrow.'

'*Ice cream!*'

'Ayah. That's what I was a thinkin'!'

Sue's eyes were shining.

'Oh, Ira – I'll bet we've got it! I'll go this minute – *no*! That won't do at all.'

'What's the matter now?'

Sue hesitated. Then she sat down on the melting snowdrift and looked at Ira with sudden resolution.

'You've got to help me, Ira. Nobody must know we ran on this – especially Dr. Barry. He's *got* to think he discovered the whole thing.'

There was a movement behind the window over their heads, but neither of them noticed it. The movement was not furtive, but the casual stir of someone arriving and sitting down at a desk. Sue's voice went on.

'It's absolutely necessary for Dr. Barry to believe that he did it. I'm going to fix it so he will. All I want you to do is tell him, when he comes to you, exactly what you've told me. But don't tell him anything else – I mean, don't tell him I've been near you, or asked you any questions. I don't mind his knowing I went to Mrs. Ventress, because I didn't find out a thing from her, but –'

'Hey, wait a minute,' said Ira quietly. 'I guess likely I know how you feel, an' all that. But it don't seem hardly fair for you to 've chased this down – if 'tis old Jud – an' I shouldn't wonder if 'twas – an' you to git no thanks for it.'

A trail of cigar smoke curled from the window above and the face of Elias Todd appeared dimly through it, his eyes alert.

'But I haven't really done anything,' said Sue. 'In a way we just stumbled on this.'

'Mebbe. But 'twas you persistin' gimme th' idea, an' the doc – '

Sue scrambled to her feet. '*No*, Ira!'

' 'Tain't fair, Miss Barton, th' way you want it!'

'It is fair!' Sue cried hotly. 'Dr. Barry's worked on this day and night – and he's losing everything. If he discovers the carrier himself, people will change their minds about him. It's terribly important for him to do it! You *must* see that, Ira! And you know perfectly well that if he thinks *I* did it he'll break his neck to see that everybody is told of it!'

Ira was silent, struggling with this confusion of loyalties and justice, while over his head, behind the barrier of glass, Elias Todd stared at Sue with a new expression – of startled respect.

'Okay,' Ira said at last. 'I'll do it your way, Miss Barton.'

Sue's face lighted with her warm smile. She took an impulsive step forward, holding out her hand.

Ira's rough, paint-spattered paw closed over it.

'I hope I'm adoin' th' right thing,' he muttered. 'How was you a figgerin' to fool th' doc about this?'

'Golly, Ira, I don't quite know. I'll have to think it out this afternoon.'

'Hm. Well, take care ye don't git a comeuppance.'

'Don't worry. It'll be all right,' said Sue, her voice ringing with assurance.

That assurance, however, lost much of its force during the afternoon. It is hard to concentrate on other matters when nursing typhoids.

Sue had only eight, it was true – since the Masons were recovering, and three of the road gang were now in Winslow Hospital as well as ten of the recent cases – and two of those remaining in Springdale were so mildly attacked that they required little attention. The eight cases, however, were scattered too far apart to make nursing them easy. Sue was discovering that being an independent Visiting Nurse was not at all as she had expected. She missed the friendly and competent supervision of a big nursing organization. There was no one to relieve her – no one to advise her. The Farm Club was merely her sponsor and knew nothing of nursing. The committee expected her to take the initiative. And though the townspeople – accustomed to having no nurse at all – were satisfied with what she was doing, Sue knew that her regular work was being neglected. She couldn't help that, under the circumstances, but she wondered how other independent nurses managed. For there were others like herself, she had discovered. New Hampshire had a good many working, as she was working, for clubs, private agencies, or hired by towns. There was no time, however, to worry about that now.

Sue returned home late and very tired to learn that Bill could not come for dinner. He had been called to Harville.

She still had not the faintest notion how she was to plant the idea of old Jud Wherity in his mind – without seeming to do so.

She ate dinner silently, not noticing that Marianna's silence was even more profound than her own. Veazie Ann looked from one to the other, and she, too, said nothing.

After dinner Marianna retired to her room with her school books, and Veazie Ann prepared to do the dishes.

'I'll wipe,' said Sue.

'Land, child, there's no need. You're tired to death already.'

'No, I'm not. I want to talk to you about something. Here! Give me that towel!'

And so, while the cold March wind whistled outside the snug kitchen and hot soapsuds made rings up Veazie Ann's plump arms, and dripping glasses shone in the lamplight, Sue wiped and talked, her thoughts clearing as she put them into words.

'That's who 'tis, sure's you're born,' Veazie Ann said.

'Yes – I'm sure of it. Everything fits – so far. Of course, there are the Masons – but Bill can go into that.' Sue paused, polishing a plate. 'Veazie Ann,' she said presently, 'how are you off for stovewood?'

'I got plenty. How come you to git to that – *oh*!' The placid face wrinkled into a smile above the dishpan. 'Land, child. You're downright quick! An' now I come to think of it I guess I *am* about out of stovewood.'

'Don't you want Bill to get a man to cut some for you?'

'Why, yes. I'd be real obliged. Maybe he could dig up old Jud Wherity for me – not but that Jud *looks* dug up any time.'

'Golly, Veazie Ann! This is marvellous. Now listen – here's what I thought we'd do –'

Sue explained and Veazie Ann nodded from time to time. 'I'm with ye, child, all the way! Shouldn't wonder 'f he's a comin' now. Want I should start in right off?'

'Yes.' Sue dropped her dish towel on a chair and flew to the door.

Bill's cheek was cold against her face for an instant. 'Hello,' he said.

'Hello, darling. Tired?'

'A bit. I had a flat tyre on the way back from Harville. How about a piece of your apple pie, Veazie Ann? Just a small piece – half a pie would do –' He grinned cheerfully at Veazie Ann, hung his coat and hat on a hook over the wood box, and put his wet gloves on the back of the stove to dry.

Veazie Ann stripped the suds from her bare arms. 'Pull right up to the table, Doctor,' she said, reaching for the roller towel. 'I got sumpthin' better'n apple pie.'

'There isn't anything. What?'

'Cold roast chicken an' baked Indian pudding – but ye don't git none without ye'll do a little chore for me.'

'Name it and it's done!' Bill pulled up a chair. 'Where's the kid?'

'Studying,' said Sue, from the rocker. She nodded at Veazie Ann – just a slight tilt of the head.

Veazie Ann's face was impassive. She disappeared into the

pantry and returned, laden. 'Here ye be, Doctor. Set to! Meanwhile here's what I want yet should do. I'm pump out of stove-wood, an' I been a tryin' for two three days to git a holt of old Jud Wherity. Wanted him to do a mite of sawing for me; but there ain't nobody laid eyes on him since th' church supper. I thought mebbe you could locate him for me.'

'Why, of course –' Bill began, and was interrupted by Sue, whose voice held a startled note.

'What do you mean, he hasn't been seen since the church supper, Veazie Ann?'

Bill turned in his chair, his eyes as startled as Sue's voice. 'Good Lord! You don't suppose the poor old devil's sick, do you – off there alone?'

'I don't know,' said Sue. 'I was wondering. Did you inoculate him, Bill?'

'Why, no,' Bill said slowly. 'I didn't. But Vinal must have.' He paused, frowning. 'No,' he went on. 'They worked from my surgery. Old Jud never showed up. To tell the truth I forgot all about him.'

'My stars!' Veazie Ann exclaimed. 'You don't suppose he's a lyin' there, struck down? Doctor! Why don't ye git a holt of Ira Prouty? He'd know 'f anybody would. He's always been kinder friendly to th' old man – gits him work on his road gang sometimes – when they figger the water bucket'll stand it, an' –'

Bill had dropped his fork. 'Did Jud Wherity work on that road gang with Ira Prouty?'

'Why, sure he did. Why?'

'Well, I didn't know it, that's all. And I don't think he ever had a Widal test. He must be the only one who didn't. My God! You don't suppose –'

'Oh, *Bill*!' Sue cried, leaping from the rocking chair. 'You – mean you think *he might be the carrier*?'

'He might,' said Bill, trying to speak calmly. 'Anyway, I'm going to find out. Veazie Ann – who saw him at the church supper?

'Why, most everybody.' Veazie Ann was vague. 'He always hangs around the back fer a dish of ice cream, an' –'

'*He does?*' Bill shouted. He was across the kitchen in two strides, and reaching for hat and coat. 'Come on, girls! Let's go!'

'Not me,' said Veazie Ann quickly. 'You two young ones go. I'll stay here and keep Marianna comp'ny when she comes down. Suz! I might's well of saved my breath to cool my porridge!'

Her last words were spoken to an empty kitchen. Sue's voice came back faintly. 'Don't wait up for me, Veazie Ann. I may be –' The rest was lost in the sudden racing of Bill's engine, outside in the dark.

Veazie Ann smiled contentedly, took a large flat key from the shelf over the sink, and began the nightly ritual of winding her great-great-grandmother's wooden clock.

14

Old Jud

THEY did as much as they could, that night. Ira Prouty, with solemn, surprised face, told Bill the story of Jud Wherity's hour of work with the road gang, while Sue thought of the strange ways of chance. If she had run over that shovel half an hour earlier Ira would have gone home, or would, perhaps, have been working again when Jud Wherity passed by. Had the incident occurred a little later, Jud himself would have been gone. In either case, he would not have stopped to ask questions, would not have been hired, and there would have been nothing for Ira to remember.

It was Bill's intention to drive out to the Ventress farm after talking to Ira, but here Sue intervened.

'I talked to Mrs. Ventress, Bill,' she said. 'I tried to do a little bit on this – as I said I would. So I went out to see her – and I didn't find out a thing. She doesn't remember what she did or who she saw – except that Lot Phinney's dog was snooping around the freezer, and that the sack covering it was lying on the step. She got Lot to take the dog away. Why don't you talk to Lot, first? *He* might have seen something.'

Lot had seen something. He had seen Jud Wherity dodging into the shadow at the back door, and he had seen two small boys – Thad Downey's sons – giggling at Jud. He had thought nothing about it at the time – nor since – until now.

'Doc!' Lot said, as nearly excited as Sue had ever seen him. 'Mebbe ye got sumpthin' by the tail. Better see them kids fust thing in the morning.'

The interview with the Downey children brought out more facts. They had been having a snow fight at the back of the town hall and had seen Mrs. Ventress give old Jud an exceedingly meagre dish of ice cream. Old Jud had eaten it sitting on the steps, and had muttered the entire time about stinginess. He had finished the ice cream, and then, as no one in authority was in sight at the moment, had helped himself to a huge second helping. He had eaten only a little of it when he heard Mrs. Ventress's voice approaching. The children giggled again, remembering.

'An' then,' Thad's oldest boy said, 'he jumped up and dumped th' hull dishful back in th' freezer an' pushed it all down with his spoon, an' skipped off. I guess he forgot to put th' sacking back, and there was ice cream all over everything. Mrs. Ventress was awful mad. She thought Lot Phinney's dog done it – but he never. He was jest a sniffin'.'

Bill reported this interview to Sue at noon, when she blew her horn outside his surgery on her way to lunch. Bill came out to the car. He was excited, she knew, for though his manner was calm enough, his eyes were almost feverishly bright. He had telephoned the Board of Health, he said, and had then gone out to Jud Wherity's shanty. Jud wasn't there – but his spring was, and Bill had taken a large bottle of water from it. The microscope had shown the water swarming with typhoid bacilli!

'But Bill!' said Sue, puzzled. 'How does it happen they didn't seep down into somebody else's water-supply? And anyway, I thought all the water had been tested.'

'Not Jud's,' Bill said, embarrassed. 'I forgot he was even in existence. I ought to be shot!'

'Yes – that would make everything so simple, wouldn't it? Honestly! But why didn't –'

'It didn't seep through very far, darling, because the soil up there happens to be sandy. If it had been clay, or rock, we'd have found the bugs farther down – but sand'll stop 'em – if there's enough sand. And there was.'

'Golly! And then what?'

'Old Dr. Vinal's coming this afternoon and we're going out there – about five. Jud ought to be home by then.'

'Poor old thing! But Bill – what about the Masons?'

'Lord! I almost forgot! I had a hunch, and saw young Bowker – he delivers the Masons' milk, you know.'

'Did you find out anything?' said Sue, who knew only too well that Jim Bowker delivered the Masons' milk.

Bill folded his arms on the car window-sill and smiled into Sue's eyes – a proud and tender smile in which he laid at her feet all that he had done, or ever hoped to do.

'Yes,' he said quietly, 'I learned something. I asked young Jim the wrong questions before. If I'd asked if he picked up anybody on the road, he'd have remembered. It seems that early one morning a long while back, he saw Jud straggling home after an all-night binge. So he picked the old man up – right in front of the Masons'. Jim says he thought he'd save himself some steps, so he handed Jud the Masons' milk bottle and asked him to take it round to the back. That's all, darling – but it was enough. The bottle was damp, and old Jud carried it round to the back door with his hand closed over the top. By the time the old lady took it in the typhoid bacilli had worked up a fine old colony.'

Sue shuddered. 'How horrible! But not bad work on your part, Dr. Barry. If you'll excuse a little rush of sentiment to the head – could I say I – I'm awfully – proud?'

Bill flushed a deep crimson. 'G'wan!' he mocked. 'I'll bet you're just cadging a dinner! And, of course, I'm always a sucker.' He touched her cheek. 'Brat!' he whispered.

Sue's eyes were very soft. 'Do I get the dinner?'

'Sure – at the Eat-a-While! Hamburgers with onion!'

'I adore hamburgers with onion!'

'Right! Oh – could you get through work in time to go out to old Jud's with us? We may need a womanly influence.'

'I'll try. I think I can finish in time. If I don't I can work a little this evening.' Sue paused. Then, 'Wouldn't it be a good idea if you took Lot Phinney along?'

'Two minds with but a single thought, my sweet. I'm going to. The town's first selectman will be a very useful witness in case of trouble.'

Sue smiled happily. Everything was going to be all right now – except for poor old Jud.

'I'm sorry for him, Bill,' she said.

'So'm I. But it can't be helped. He mustn't be allowed to go on like this. Can you meet me here at five?'

'I think so. But if I'm not here in time, go without me.'

Sue tried to hurry that afternoon, but it was difficult, for while her home nurses were doing splendidly there were always unexpected things cropping up. The routine nursing, of course, she no longer had to do, as far as the typhoids were concerned. Sue was a good and patient instructor, and nowadays she always found her typhoids in fresh beds – the soiled linen kept carefully separate from other laundry. Patients' dishes had their own pan and were usually boiling merrily on the kitchen stove when Sue arrived. Patients' mouths were clean. Thermometers were neat in little glasses filled with alcohol. A table was always spread with newspapers, ready for her bag.

But today was an off day, it seemed. Sue found one patient with a tell-tale red mark at the base of his spine – a mark which did not go away when the patient was turned on his side. This was a sure sign of an incipient bedsore and Sue worked long and hard on it – massaging it first with alcohol, then with cocoa butter. Then she must improvise the equivalent of a rubber air ring, which she accomplished by twisting a small sheet into a roll and winding it with bandages. This would keep the patient's weight off the treacherous red mark.

Her next typhoid was running a very high temperature. The family would not have Bill under any circumstances, and Dr. Vinal was goodness knows where. Sue gave the patient an alcohol rub – a long one and a very cold one, and was gratified to find that she had brought the temperature down two degrees.

Then there was a case of influenza with a pounding headache. An ice-cap was the solution – but where was she to get an ice-cap on a mountain farm? There wasn't even a hot-water bottle. The family was well-to-do, but they were Spartan. They didn't hold with foolishness like them little rubber hot-water bottles. Grannie's old stone jug was good enough for them – or a hot stone. And they'd never heard of an ice-cap.

'But you can't rest a stone jug full of ice on poor Bijah's head,' Sue protested. 'Let's see – would you have an old inner tube? I might do something with that.'

They had an old inner tube – and Sue did very well with it, thanks to the New England farmer's habit of doing his own tyre-patching. She cut a ten-inch piece of tubing, glued one end together with rubber cement, folded it over twice, and gummed the folds tightly with a wide strip of tyre-patching. Then she filled the tube with ice, and rolled the open end over a stout piece of wire after the manner of the old-fashioned curler. The whole made an excellent ice-cap – but Sue's watch hands stood at ten minutes to five when she left.

There was no use in going to Bill's surgery now. She'd better drive straight out to Jud's – if she could find the shanty. It was somewhere off the road beyond Martha Edgett's sprawling farm. Probably Mrs. Edgett could tell her.

Mrs. Edgett could and did. 'You go on up the road a piece,' she said, standing in the kitchen doorway. 'When you come to a turn – the second turn, 'tis – leave your car – ye can't git no farther in it – and foller the little path to the right, straight up the mountain. What's the matter with old Jud? He sick?'

Sue evaded the question. 'Dr. Barry just said he'd like me to come up there around five, if I had time.'

Mrs. Edgett's thin nervous features relaxed in a smile. 'Guess you ain't had much time lately for anything,' she said. ' ''Twas a lucky day for us when we give you this job. I dunno where we'd of ben without you. The Club's real pleased. They ben a readin' of your reports, an' I guess they got a new idea of nurses. Well, I mustn't keep you. Hyper along now – before my tongue gits to goin'.'

Sue 'hypered'.

She found the path without difficulty, for Bill's car stood beside it, off the road. Sue parked just beyond and trudged up the mountain side through a soup of mud and slush. The bare branches of alders caught at her as she scrambled upwards, and she noted, for the first time, that their buds were swelling. Spring really was here, she thought, though the snow was still deep, in the woods. She turned once, to look back through a frame of branches at the mountains, rising wave upon motionless wave beyond the valley. They, too, wore their coat of snow, but it was thinning. Their watercourses were veined with brown, and great rounds of granite lifted naked grey backs to the sun.

'I haven't noticed them for a long time,' Sue realized. 'I've been so buried in work.' The thought turned her back to the path again.

Old Jud's shanty lay half-way down the other side of a rise, and Sue caught a glimpse of movement through the trees. Bill, Dr. Vinal, and Lot Phinney stood before the closed door of the shanty. Dr. Vinal's voice came back on the wind.

'Come on out of there, Jud. You're caught, and you know it!'

Sunlight glinted on the shanty's tin patchwork, on the pyramid of empty beer cans beside a rabbit hutch. Chickens fluttered uneasily in huddled coops. There was no sound from the cabin.

Lot Phinney's irritable voice joined Dr. Vinal's.

'Come on, ye tarnation old fool! Ye want I should hev ye up for resistin' th' law?'

A stream of shrieking profanity poured from the cabin and Sue flushed, but she came on steadily. This was no time to pay attention to mere words. The men heard her step and turned, Bill's eyes lighting.

'Shut up, you scummudglon!' Lot Phinney roared suddenly at the cabin. 'There's a lady present!'

The voice disposed of ladies in one blistering sentence.

'Mr. Wherity!' Sue called. 'It's Miss Barton, the nurse. Would you let me come in?'

'No, I wun't!' mimicked the voice in an unpleasant falsetto.

'Fust one that tries to git in this door gits a bullet in th' puss.'

Sue's face went white. 'Has he got a *gun*?' she whispered to Bill.

'I don't know,' he returned. 'He says he has. Don't worry, sweet.' Then, to the other men, 'I think I'll have a try at this, boys. Arguing doesn't seem to work.'

'For the Lord's sake, Doc!' Lot Phinney exclaimed. 'What ye goin' to do?'

'Just go in.'

'No! No, boy!' Dr. Vinal said. 'Wait a minute! Maybe we can —'

But Bill was already moving towards the closed door. The two men watched him, fascinated. Then, with one accord, they moved forward behind him. Sue stood motionless, the back of her hand pressed against her mouth, a tightness in her throat.

Bill's tall figure halted before the door to listen. Then he remarked pleasantly, 'This is tough luck, Jud, but we can't help it any more than you can. There's no use trying to dodge it — you'll have to have an examination and a blood test. Better open the door.'

'Ye ain't a goin' to tech me!' Jud shrieked. '*Doctors!* Lyin', sneakin' quacks! Givin' folks typhoid fever, an' a blamin' it on an old man!' There was a cackle of laughter. 'Ye don't fool me! I showed ye up! Fine big sign, 'twas, all over yer car! *Quack.* An' I told 'em all about ye. They'll run ye out of town! Said they would!'

'Brace up, feller! Getting sore isn't going to stop anything.'

'*Tech that door an' I'll shoot!*'

'Go right ahead,' said Bill easily, and set his shoulder against the flimsy wood. It gave way with a splintering crash to reveal the grimy figure of Jud Wherity crouched behind an overturned table, his red-rimmed eyes glassy with fright.

Bill pushed the table aside with his foot. 'Come on, old man,' he said, his voice gentle with pity. 'Stand up now, and take off your coat.'

'Wh-what ye goin' to do with me?'

'Nothing right now – except make an examination. But tomorrow we're going to take you over to the County Farm, where you'll have three good meals a day and a comfortable bed at night.'

'Ye – ain't goin' to put me in no jail?'

'No.'

There were tears in the red-rimmed eyes.

Slowly the old man rose to his feet and his trembling hands crept towards the first button on his coat.

'*Well!*' said Dr. Vinal in the doorway.

Lot Phinney, beside him, drew a long breath. 'Well!' he drawled. 'The durned old coot was a bluffin'! He never had no gun at all!'

Sue made a faint sound. Lot wheeled to look at her and sprang forward. 'Take it easy, girl! Ye all right?'

'Oh, yes!' said Sue, through stiff lips. 'I'm j-just dandy!'

Lot put a fatherly arm round her.

'There now –' he said.

'I – I'm all right, really. I – just had a bad moment.' Her eyes went to Bill in pride and relief. 'Wh-what can you do with a – an idiot like that?'

'I dunno what you'll make out to do, but I know what *I'm* a goin' to do – the town's goin' to hear about this, an' hear plenty!'

15

Two and two make four

THE town did hear plenty. Before seven o'clock it had learned all the facts and had invented twice as many more. It was said that Bill had been working for months tracking down the carrier. It was said that he had not had to work at all, but had dreamed three nights running of old Jud Wherity, and the truth had come to him like 'twas the finger of the Lord a pointin'. Mrs. Ventress, on hearing that the carrier had been found, was reported as saying strangely that she had known all along, and she hoped the authorities would make short work of the dog.

Accounts of the scene at Jud Wherity's shack grew in drama as they spread. Old Jud had frothed at the mouth and fallen down in a fit when confronted by Dr. Barry. Bill had battered down the whole front of the shanty to get in, and old Jud had shot at him steadily the entire time. The cabin had been an arsenal of machine-guns. Bill had found a paper under Jud's pillow, with a list of names on it – all those crossed off being the names of persons now ill with typhoid. Old Jud was in the pay of a foreign country and strange winking lights had been seen in the vicinity of his shanty on the night of the church supper. Bill was said to have flung open the door of the shack and cried in ringing tones, 'I do not fear your bullets, Jud Wherity! I have come to save the people of Springdale!' Sue was reported to have fainted dead away. She had been saved from instant death by her Henry Street bag. The bag was said to be riddled with bullet holes. Lot Phinney and Dr. Vinal had climbed in a back window and seized Jud just as he was turning a machine-gun on Bill. The noise of the battle had been heard clear at Martha Edgett's. In fact, there were even people in Springdale who said they had heard the sound of distant shots.

Sue and Bill, arriving at the Eat-a-While in Sue's car – Bill's was left at his surgery – found themselves the centre of excitement. People waved at the car as it passed and crowded into the Eat-a-While to shake Bill's hand, saying they'd known all along that he'd outsmart Jud Wherity – and no one saw anything peculiar in this statement. Ex-patients paused in the doorway, hesitated, and came in to remark sheepishly that they had boils or sore throats or infected fingers and if'n the doc was to be in his surgery ter-morrer they'd like to drop in for a look-over.

'How's your practice, Doctor?' Sue murmured through her hamburger and onions.

'Coming up!' Bill grinned, his eyes bright with happiness.

Small boys cheered the car on its way out of town – a town suddenly beautiful to Sue and Bill. Lights twinkled all up the pleasant valley. The river chuckled among its stones. A gay little moon outlined serene peaks.

'You know,' Sue remarked suddenly, 'I believe old Jud is actually looking forward to the County Farm. Seems strange, doesn't it?'

'Oh, I don't know. He's old and tired, and sick of shifting for himself, and bewildered by all this typhoid business which he can't grasp. He knows he'll be comfortable there, and he's probably thankful at heart. He admitted when I was examining him that he had been badly frightened by his encounter with the medical authorities, and he was apparently very foggy in his mind about the business of being a typhoid carrier. He simply knew that he wanted to be left alone, that he hated the whole tribe of doctors, and that he wanted no new ones in the vicinity of Harville.'

They drove on in silence until the lights of Veazie Ann's cottage gleamed through the trees and the sound of the car brought two excited figures to the door – one stout and motherly, one young and wide-eyed.

'My stars!' Veazie Ann clutched Sue. 'Be you all right? We heard you was shot!'

'Of course I'm all right!' Sue laughed. 'Nobody was shot – not even a gun. Why, Marianna! You've been crying!'

'I ain't! I got a cold!' Marianna denied. 'What happened, Sue? Le's see your bag? They said it was fulla holes! Did Bill really knock that guy down with a rabbit?'

'With a *what?*'

'A rabbit! They said old Jud come at him and Bill grabbed a rabbit outa a hutch an' swung it round his head an' —'

'Good heavens!' Sue moaned.

'Well, come in, both of ye,' said Veazie Ann. 'Ye can tell about it around the stove just's good's ye can tell it up to your necks in slush. My land, Sue! Your feet's sopping wet! I never — *who's this?*'

'This' was a long black limousine driven by a uniformed chauffeur. It rolled to a stop behind Bill's car and the chauffeur got out, carrying a large basket.

'I'm looking for Miss Barton,' he said to the astonished group in the doorway.

'I'm Miss Barton.'

The chauffeur touched his cap. 'Compliments of Mr. Todd,' he said, and offered Sue the basket.

She took it from him and, being unprepared for its weight, nearly dropped it.

'Why — er — thank you,' she said, finding her voice. 'I mean — please thank Mr. Todd.'

'Very good, miss.' The chauffeur turned smartly on his heel and disappeared into the shadow of his car.

'Gee!' Marianna almost shouted. 'Bring it in quick, Sue! Maybe it's orchids!'

'No orchid ever weighed this much,' said Sue, 'unless it was solid gold!'

Bill sprang to take the basket, and they followed him inside, where he set his burden on the kitchen table and stood back for Sue.

The basket was very new and the cover came up stiffly. Marianna and Veazie Ann crowded close, staring. Bill peered over Sue's shoulder.

There was a moment of astounded silence as a black-and-white dachshund puppy rose up timidly from the depths of the basket and placed a brown glove-like paw on the rim. Dark almond eyes, worried and questioning, went from face to face.

'*Oh!*' Sue cried softly. '*The darling!*' Her hand went out to the domed little head, fingers caressing behind the long ears.

The puppy responded instantly with eyes and tail. It scrabbled, begging to be taken up – to be comforted in this strange place. Sue lifted it out and it burrowed in her arms. 'Oh!' she said again, and a wet nose touched her chin – a timid, pleading little nose.

'Lord! What a beauty!' Bill said. 'Look, Sue! It's got an envelope on its collar.'

'Oh, lem*me*! Please!' Marianna cried, and added surprisingly – to the puppy – 'Did it was!'

The puppy's eyes followed her, but it clung to Sue while Marianna unfastened the envelope and drew out a paper and a card which she read aloud, stumbling over the difficult names.

The paper was an American Kennel Club registration and stated that Maxl von Neurenheim, male, dachshund, aged 4 months, was the son of Champion Tristan of Zuzu and Champion Leisal von Wullff, whose further ancestries were enumerated with impersonal respect.

Bill whistled, speechless, and Veazie Ann said faintly, 'My land!'

The card read simply:

> *For Miss Sue Barton*
> *From Elias P. Todd*
> *Congratulations!*

'Congratulations?' said Bill, puzzled, looking at Sue.

She stared at him blankly. 'But how *funny*,' she said, clasping the puppy. 'What do you suppose he means by that? Congratulations for what?'

A look of startled comprehension flickered in Veazie Ann's shrewd eyes. It vanished instantly.

'Shouldn't wonder,' she remarked, 'if he'd had kind of a change of heart about ye, Sue. Likely he's heard tell how ye've worked all through the epidemic, and feels kinder foolish 'twarn't him give ye th' job.'

'Oh.' Sue accepted the explanation at once.

Bill grinned. 'Anyway,' he said, 'the old boy certainly makes handsome amends.'

It was not until later that night, after Sue and Marianna had returned from driving Bill home, and Sue was comfortably in bed, that Veazie Ann knocked at the door and came in.

'My land!' she said. 'Look at him! Burrowin' kind of critter, ain't he?'

The puppy, refusing to sleep in his basket or be separated by so much as an inch from Sue, had pushed himself under the extra quilt on the foot of the bed. Only his black, scythe-like tail was visible.

'Took to ye right off, didn't he?' Veazie Ann went on.

Sue laughed. 'That's because I was the one who took him out of the basket. He thinks I rescued him from a fate worse than death – so now I have to be his mother.'

Veazie Ann's amused eyes rested for an instant on the helpless tail. Then they returned to Sue. 'Where,' she said, 'did you'n' Ira Prouty have your little confab?'

Sue put down her book. 'Why – why, up at Bald Trail Inn – Veazie Ann! You – you don't *think* –'

'Warn't any doors or windows open handy, was they?'

Sue's bright head stirred on the pillow. 'I – I didn't notice any.' She sat up. 'You don't suppose he heard –'

I ain't supposin' nothin'. But two and two made four when *I* was at school. Guess likely they still do – you an' Ira Prouty – Bald Trail Inn and Elias Todd. That's four, ain't it? Good night, child. Hope the little scamp don't keep ye awake.'

'*Veazie Ann! Wait!*'

But Veazie Ann had gone.

16

Marianna

SUE wrote to Elias Todd the next day – a warmly appreciative note of thanks for the puppy. She naturally didn't ask what he meant by congratulating her, for if he had meant what Veazie Ann had suggested, the less said about it the better.

'And now,' she thought, as the envelope vanished into the letter box at the Post Office, 'perhaps we can all settle down to work, in peace and quiet.'

It was a reasonable assumption, certainly. The panic was over. Bill's practice was on the way to recovery. The typhoid patients, though only beginning convalescence, would require less and less of Sue's time, and she could turn her attention to other work. She was aware, of course, that Marianna was being persistently moody and sullen, and that her English was going from bad to worse, but Marianna had always been unpredictable. It didn't occur to Sue that the matter was serious.

She blamed herself bitterly, afterwards, for her lack of perception. 'I ought to have *seen* –' she told herself. But she didn't see, and Veazie Ann, supposing that Marianna was normally 'just dretful odd', said nothing. It was Kit's arrival in mid-April which shattered the false calm, for Kit saw what was happening and brought the matter to a climax.

Until then, however, Sue and Bill did have a happy interval of work together, undisturbed by outside considerations – the kind of work they had dreamed of doing.

The people of Springdale and of the surrounding villages and farms were becoming as enthusiastically for Bill as they had been enthusiastically against him. Sue's cases increased proportionately, and though she rarely had time to go with Bill on his visits they went over the cases together in the evenings, reporting their findings, discussing symptoms and treatment. Springdale expectant mothers, coming to Bill for examination, were persuaded by Sue – with some difficulty – to attend a Mothers' Club, where they would be taught what to eat to have a healthy baby, what to wear, what clothes to make for the coming child, and the best-proved methods of taking care of it when it arrived. Several times Sue was wakened in the night by a hurried but cheerful Bill and drove with him to some lonely farm to bring a new and indignant human being into the world – a squalling red mite which Sue oiled and dressed in the oven of the kitchen stove, by the light of a kerosene lamp; Bill, meanwhile, sustaining the trembling-kneed young father with hearty male conversation.

When it was all over they drove back to Springdale through the grey dawn, sometimes talking, sometimes in a companionable silence. Their tired but contented young eyes watched more than one sunrise over the mountains while the car toiled through mud, floundered in ruts, and splashed through streams. Maxl von Neurenheim slumbered under his blanket on the jolting back seat on all these trips. Sue took him wherever she went, leaving him in the car while she made her visits. He was an odd little dog – a strange combination of gaiety and pessimism, charmingly affectionate with known friends, insultingly suspicious of everyone else. Apparently he believed every stranger guilty of the most horrible crimes until each was proved innocent beyond the shadow of a doubt.

'I don't know where he gets such ideas,' Sue told Bill. 'I wouldn't be caught dead repeating what he thinks people think!'

Bill grinned. 'A fine companion for my future wife! If my Airedale hadn't died of old age he'd have taught that young princeling what's what.'

'I don't want him changed at all!' said Sue, outraged, and Bill shouted with laughter.

So the happy, work-filled days slipped away into April. Snow was still deep in the mountain ravines, where there would be ski-ing until June, but the valleys and meadows were bare and the streams began to roar among their boulders.

Sue discarded the faithful but heavy raccoon coat for the one she had worn at Henry Street – a grey-green tweed which was lighter and more comfortable. She was away early, for calls came either directly to her at Veazie Ann's or by way of Bill on the telephone. She did not have to stop at his surgery.

She found the work very different from the work she had done at Henry Street – not in regard to methods or individual cases, for influenza and measles are influenza and measles whether on New York's crowded East Side or on a lonely, wind-swept mountain farm. The difference lay in her utter aloneness in her work; in the stubborn independence of the people, who were horrified at the thought of being sick away from home, and did not want organizations to do anything about them.

The nurses working in or near cities, or in industrial centres among a foreign-born people, did not have this problem. But the people of Springdale and the surrounding villages were native to their deepest roots, and almost more than they were native they were fiercely local in their pride and interests, fiercely individual in their independence. What the problems of other visiting nurses in New Hampshire might be, or whether her own were unique to Springdale, Sue didn't know. Her position was clearly enough defined. She was the local Visiting Nurse. She went wherever she was needed. She did whatever the occasion demanded. She had no supervisor but Bill and her own conscience. Springdale didn't want to be organized. It simply wanted a nurse when sick, and that was all there was to it. The people wouldn't go to rest cures or sanatoriums or city specialists. They wouldn't go to clinics because the clinics were too far away. They *would* go to Winslow's small hospital, but only when they were desperately ill. They were, in fact, a gigantic clan of furious individualists. But there was plenty of work for Sue, and her fees made up at least 75 per cent of her salary, now. She could scarcely keep up with her cases – scattered as they were over miles of country. But somehow she managed to go with the silent Marianna to the cinema once or twice a week.

'Why don't you have some of the girls from school for dinner?' Sue asked once.

Marianna shrugged. 'Too much trouble,' she said.

'Why? Veazie Ann wouldn't mind. She likes a lot going on.'

'Sure, I know she does. I meant *I* don't wanta bother.'

'Oh,' said Sue, and let this subject drop. If Marianna didn't want to bother she *wouldn't* bother, and there was no use in trying to persuade her. She remembered now that Veazie Ann had said that the high-school students hadn't been particularly cordial to Marianna, but in matters of that kind Marianna was amply able to take care of herself. It wasn't very strange that Marianna had made no friends among the girls of her own age. She had made none in New York.

Sue wondered sometimes if Marianna were interested in any of the boys at school, and finally ventured to inquire. She was promptly informed that Marianna had no use for boys – never had and never would – and even if she was *crazy* about 'em she wouldn't look at these hicks. All they thought about was farms and football.

Sue did not bring up that subject again!

'I'm terribly sorry that I'm away so much,' she told Marianna one evening on the way home from a film. 'I – I didn't expect to be when I wrote asking you to come. This typhoid epidemic upset everything. But we're getting more organized now. I ought to have a lot more time this summer, and then we'll have fun. Kit will be here, and –'

'Oh, don't worry about me, Sue. I know it ain't your fault. You've been swell. It's just –' She paused.

'Just – what?' Sue asked, manoeuvring the car round a deep rut.

'Oh, I – hey! Look out for that rock! Geeze! There goes your tyre! It's all right, Maxl – you ain't dead yet!'

Sue stopped the car and got out. 'It *is* all right,' she said.

'It's bruised a little, but nothing worse. If you'll give me a hand we might roll this stone out of the way before somebody else hits it.'

Whatever Marianna had been about to say was not revealed, then or later. She seemed to have forgotten it, for when they got back into the car she gathered Maxl into her lap and began casually, 'Kit decided what day she's coming?'

'Not definitely. I suppose in another week or so, if she's going to have any holiday before she starts this new job on the first of May.'

'Think she'll like it?'

'Of course! She'll adore it!'

'Mm,' said Marianna, and that was all.

Kit arrived in Springdale the last week in April – having spent the previous week with her family, in Canada. She was happy and excited – about her new work, about seeing the girls again, about being in the country once more, about Maxl, about Veazie Ann.

Everything interested her, from the spectacular beauty of the White Mountains to the last detail of the typhoid epidemic. Her brown eyes shone; her eyebrows were raised in constant lively inquiry; her laughter rang through Veazie Ann's old house. She was like a strong, fresh breeze blowing the dust of weariness from Sue's mind, bringing laughter to Marianna's sullen mouth, stirring Bill to dramatic tales of the life of a country doctor. Maxl was charmed with her. Veazie Ann, caught up in this stimulating atmosphere of appreciation, was drawn into accounts of the Springdale of fifty years ago, and of her courtship by the defunct Mr. Cooney.

'Well, my land,' she said defensively to Sue, 'Miss Van asks so many questions – an' the funny thing is, she really wants to know. She makes you feel like you're an awful interestin' person. It's a kind of gift.' She added suddenly, 'You got one, too, that's jest as good.'

'I have?'

'Sartin'! Where Miss Van makes folks feel all het up and

interestin', you git 'em to feelin' it don't make no odds whether they're interestin' or not – they got a friend, anyway.'

'Why, Veazie Ann!' said Sue, touched. 'What a lovely thing to say!'

Veazie Ann smiled. 'There ye be,' she said, 'a doin' of it to me.'

'But I *am* your friend!'

'That's what I mean. It's real. That's what gits folks. Look at your patients a swearin' by ye – an' Lot Phinney, and Ira Prouty, and Martha Edgett –'

Mention of Martha Edgett reminded Sue that she must turn in her reports, and that Kit would surely want to go with her. Kit wanted to go everywhere and meet everybody, and her week's visit was so filled with goings and comings and laughter and talk that it seemed no longer than a day.

Kit, however, had not been too absorbed to notice Marianna's grim silences, and towards the end of the week, on Sue's afternoon off, she took the matter in hand – coming back from a trip to Winslow, where Sue had taken her to be interviewed by the hospital trustees.

'Look here, Sue,' she began as the car toiled up the first mountain grade on the road home, 'what's the matter with Marianna? She behaves like chief mourner at a wake.'

'I don't know,' said Sue absently, eyes on the narrow winding road. 'I guess she's bored, poor kid. She doesn't make friends easily – and I've been so rushed –'

'For heaven's sake, Bat! Wake up! She isn't bored – she's in a state of furious resentment. She's boiling. You can't stay five minutes in the same room with her without looking for a screen in case she blows up before you can get out.'

'*Kit!*' Sue was shocked. 'Are you positive about that? I know she's been offish lately, but –'

'Offish! Don't be an idiot! She's practically murderous!' Kit added more gently. 'I know you've been in a state with all this mess, but honestly I don't see how you could help noticing!

Haven't you seen how she's changed? She used to *try*, at least, to speak decent English. Now she talks as badly as she did when she came to us. She's gone right back. She's sulky and bitter and –'

'And I've been an awful fool, I suppose,' said Sue miserably.

'You certainly have! Come on, now, start concentrating. When did all this begin – or don't you know?'

'Why – well, I don't, I'm afraid. She was scared stiff of the country when she first came, but she seemed to get over that. Veazie Ann said the kids at school didn't like her much – but that wouldn't bother Marianna.'

'No, it's not that,' Kit said slowly. 'We'd better find out, Sue.'

The session with Marianna took place that evening. She had retired upstairs with her books immediately after dinner and presently Sue and Kit followed her, little Maxl pattering earnestly at Sue's heels.

Marianna had the slope-ceilinged bedroom opposite Sue's. The door was closed when the girls came upstairs and they exchanged uneasy glances.

'This is going to be Something,' Kit whispered.

Sue knocked on the door. 'Hey, there!' she called. 'Could you bear a little company?'

'Sure.' Marianna's voice was gruff. Her steps, once hearty and bounding, came slowly and heavily across the room to the door. It opened and Marianna confronted them, her stocky figure wrapped in a dressing-gown. 'C'mon in,' she said pleasantly, and returned to her seat by the window.

The girls climbed up on the vast feather bed, laughing as they sank into its depths. Maxl watched them with bright disapproving eyes and then, since no one offered to help him up, withdrew, outraged, to sit at Marianna's feet. She bent down to pat him. There was an instant of silence.

'Well,' Kit said brightly. 'My job is settled, anyway. I wished you'd got out of school in time to come with us, Marianna. It's a gorgeous drive.'

Marianna lifted Maxl to her lap and nodded gloomily. She made no other reply.

Sue watched her, with a sinking sensation. 'I certainly have been slow,' she thought. 'She's as grim as the Old Man of the Mountains.'

Sue had meant to lead up to her inquiry gradually, after a reasonable amount of chatter, but this she now realized was impossible. Marianna wasn't chattering. Her eyes had the old hard look; she was a little pale, and her brown hair stood out in wiry defiance all over her head. Only her hands were gentle, playing with Maxl's long ears.

The girls stirred uncomfortably. Kit was sitting cross-legged in a deep hollow, her expression one of forced lightness, her brown eyes troubled. Sue leaned back against the pillows, slim and vivid, her delicate features wistful with anxiety and contrition – for the brief moment before she sat up and spoke with determination.

"Is anything worrying you, Marianna?' she said bluntly. 'Are you all right at school?'

Marianna shrugged. 'Yeah. I guesso.'

'Then what is it? I know there's something. Won't you please tell us? Has anything happened?'

Marianna's head was bent over the little dog curled in her lap. When she looked up she looked straight at Sue with desperate honesty.

'Maybe I'd better tell you,' she said. 'I – I wasn't gointer till after the school year was over. I didn't wanter upset you right now. You been havin' it kinder tough.'

'But what's *happened*, honey?'

'There ain't nothin' happened – except I don't like it here. I wanter go back to New York. I guess I ain't cut out for the country.'

There was a pause. Then Kit said gently, 'Why don't you like it, Marianna? I mean – is there any *special* reason – has anybody been rotten to you, or –'

'Nope. And I wouldn't care if they was! It – it – I *hate* the country!' Her voice was rising a little and she made a visible effort to control it. 'You been swell to me – both of you. You – you done a lot for me. But I can't stay in no dump like this.' Her lips quivered and she swallowed. Maxl stared up at her, frightened. Marianna set him on the floor and stood up.

'Wait a minute, kid,' said Sue. 'Are you *sure* you want to go back to the city?'

'*Am I sure?* Cripes!' She faced Sue, rigid with emotion. 'D'you think I'm just doin' this for fun? I hate them great mountains, an' th' stillness, an' the silly kids at school – they don't know nothin' – an' th' snow, an' the noises at night, an' all these dumb people, an' –'

'Hey!' Kit said. 'These people aren't dumb. They're fine! If you'd stop thinking so much about yourself and take a little trouble to –'

Sue's warning glance stopped her.

'But Marianna,' Sue said, 'you'll be going over to Winslow to do your training, and then –'

'*I ain't goin' to be a nurse!*' Marianna said through clenched teeth.

The girls stared at her, aghast.

'Then – what are you – going to do?' Sue asked at last.

'I'm goin' back to New York soon's school's out! I'm goin' to finish the year like I come here to do! An' then I scram! I seen enough of nursing! There ain't anything to it! I done all right before, in New York. I can go back an' do all right again!'

Sue's voice was even. 'All right, my dear. Of course you shall go back if you feel like that. But how about thinking it over first? There's no –'

'I been thinking about it till I'm goofy!'

'But I haven't. I didn't realize. I think we ought to talk about it first. Please sit down, like a dear, will you?' Sue smiled into the frantic young face. 'You make me feel all dithery, seething at me like that. And Maxl's going out to shoot himself in another minute.'

Marianna grinned faintly and boosted Maxl up on the bed.

Some of the tension had gone from her face when she sat down.

In the silence that followed – not an awkward silence now, but a thinking silence – Marianna stared at the toe of her bedroom slipper, Kit leaned impassively against a bedpost, and Sue stroked Maxl's long sleekness. The little dog was dimly aware of something wrong and pressed against Sue, his bright eyes going from face to face.

Sue was thinking hard. She should never have brought Marianna out of the city, but she *had* brought her, and that was that. So now what? If Marianna gave up all thought of becoming a nurse and returned to New York alone she would return to her old ways as she had already returned to her former speech. There would be no more schooling – except of the wrong kind, for in a year's time she'd be a first-class shoplifter. She'd been well started on that road before, and when jobs proved scarce – as they would – she would help herself to what she wanted. It would be little things at first – clothes, a pair of shoes, a bit of jewellery. Then she'd find it could be sold and the rebel Marianna would go from bad to worse along the path that has only one ending – the gates of the State Penitentiary.

Sue took a deep breath and Maxl peered into her face, his tail quivering in doubt and distress.

'It's all right, baby,' she said to him. But it was not all right and even Maxl knew it. Marianna *must not* go back to the city on her own. Somehow she must be kept here.

Sue looked up at last, assuming an expression of pleasant, impersonal friendliness.

'Well,' she said, 'I've thought. And of course you shall go back. But I wish you'd agree to one thing –'

'What?' Marianna's tone was hostile for the first time.

'I wish you'd wait till the autumn.'

'*No!*'

'Now hold on a minute! Summer is coming and you know darned well that you can't pick jobs off city trees in summer. In

the autumn I'll get you a job, somehow, through Henry
Street –'

'I can get my own job!'

'Sure you can – but I can get you a better one, and try and
laugh *that* off! But I can't get it in summer. Besides, no matter
how much you hate the country you've got to admit that it'll
be cool. New York is a roasting, sizzling furnace in summer.
Heat – no money – no job! Do be reasonable, lamb. Stick it out
just this summer. The time isn't right to go now. That's all I'm
asking.'

'I don't care how hot the city is – and I'd rather sleep under
the overhead railway any time than be squashed by all these
mountains. And I can always get money by –' She broke off
abruptly.

Sue thought, 'She *means* to go back to all that –' Aloud she
said calmly, 'If you're going to be all right you're going to be
all right. So why not begin to be it in the autumn?'

'Because –'

Kit broke in. She had remained silent up to this point. Now
she said crisply, 'See here, Marianna, this is all very dramatic
and independent and all that, but it's a rotten thing to do to
Sue – and me too, for that matter.'

'I don't see why –' Marianna began hotly.

'I'm going to tell you why if you'll give me a chance. You
owe something to both of us – oh, *not* money, for *goodness'*
sake – you owe us some loyalty and co-operation. All Sue asked
you to do was to wait until the autumn, and even if you think
there's no point in it, it wouldn't hurt you to do it. There's
nothing difficult about it – except the difficulties you make
yourself. Summer *isn't* any time to try to make a new start in
New York, and we'd feel a lot easier in our minds if you'd
wait.'

Marianna's face was crimson. 'But that's silly,' she began. 'I
can take care of mysel' –'

'Call it silly if you like! It doesn't really matter what you call
it. The point is that Sue asked you to do this – and it's the

first time she's *ever* asked you to do anything you didn't want to do. I think you might –'

'Okay!' Marianna said violently. 'If that's how you look at it I'll stay. Nobody ain't gonna say I'm a louse! But there's one thing – if I stick around this dump till –'

'October,' Kit said quickly.

Marianna swallowed. 'All right – October! *Then* I can go back without no fuss?'

'Absolutely,' said Sue, making no effort to keep the relief out of her voice. 'You're a darling, Marianna!'

'Aw!' said Marianna crossly.

17

Summer

'GOLLY!' Kit said. 'What a business! But anyway, you've got until October –'

'Thanks to you.'

'Got anything special in mind?'

'Yes – and no.' Sue reached for the poker and prodded the coals in Veazie Ann's front-room fire. Bill usually did that for her. The evenings seemed very bleak without him, but it couldn't be helped. Sue supposed she ought to be glad he was so busy – and she *was* glad, she told herself. If only his evenings with her hadn't been reduced to two or three a week.

The fire in the grate snapped briskly. Sue stood the poker in its corner and leaned back in the big wing chair. 'I haven't any but a general plan,' she went on. 'After all – I've only had about half an hour to think about it. The only thing I can see to do is to keep Marianna busy all summer. I'll take her with me all the time – and if she thinks nursing is just a lower form of manicuring she'll have a chance to find out differently.'

'I hope so! I didn't like that!'

Kit hitched the footstool on which she was sitting a little farther from the stove.

'You're telling me! Not that anybody wants to make her be a nurse if she doesn't want to be one. The thing is, she did want to – until she got the wrong idea of it. And it's the only real ambition she seems to have had. If she gives up the idea of nursing she'll just pop off down the drain – which would be an awful pity! There's good stuff in Marianna.' Sue stared at the fire for a moment. Then, 'Maybe you noticed I didn't faint away, or start eating the wallpaper, when she said she wasn't going to be a nurse?'

'I did! That was bright of you, Bat. If you don't make an

issue of it, so that she gets that iron will of hers set against it, you may have a chance. But listen! I've got an idea! As soon as I'm settled in the Winslow Hospital, bring her over. She's never been inside a hospital, and it *might* –'

'*Good girl!*'

The visit to the hospital, however, was not a success. Possibly Marianna suspected the reason why the girls showed her over the buildings with such care. In any case, she made the rounds of the wards and operating-room with polite impassiveness, inspected Kit's pleasant suite of rooms without comment, and eyed the trim young nurses with almost open contempt.

'Kinder like the army, ain't it?' she remarked to Sue. 'They gotta take orders from everybody.'

'Why not?' Sue asked pleasantly. 'The people who give the orders know their jobs. The kids are just learning theirs. And the work's terribly interesting.'

'Huh! Making beds and washing people!'

So it was Sue, instead of Marianna, who was really affected by the visit. The smell of soapsuds and antiseptics, the sound of rubber-soled feet on tiled floors, the sight of the orderly sunlit wards with their white rows of beds, brought Sue an unexpected nostalgia. She longed for the hurry, the fun, the clocklike co-ordination of work, the sense of being a part of an important institution. One had all that in some measure in any branch of nursing, but Sue's work, now, was done alone. And it wasn't, she realized, at all the same thing.

'I *wish*,' she burst out to Marianna on the way back to Springdale, 'that Bill had a hospital! It would be so marvellous!'

Marianna said nothing – a habit she showed no signs of discontinuing.

'She's promised she'll stay until October,' Sue told Kit the following week-end, 'and she'll stay if it kills her –'

'But she's going to make the worst of it.'

'Exactly. I'll be glad when school is over in June. *Then*, maybe I can do something with her!'

'*Maybe*,' Kit said doubtfully, but Sue was very sure.

It was in the hope of arousing Marianna's interest in local nursing problems that Sue began to talk more, at home, about her work.

One nurse, in this passionately individualized community, she said, could do little except teach bedside nursing, be on hand for emergencies, and carry out doctor's orders. What was needed badly was instruction in sanitation and hygiene. The State Nursing Association was co-operating in every way possible – sending Sue quantities of Public Health bulletins for distribution, offering her its nurses' consultation service, inviting her to meetings. But it could do little else to help her with her immediate problem of how to extend really effective instruction to the scattered farm population.

'If we had our own hospital,' Bill said, 'we could do something.'

'How? What?'

'Well, in the first place it would be *their* hospital. It would lend a certain importance to the community. They'd be proud of it, as they are of the Consolidated School. It would be a darned tiny medical centre, but it would *be* a medical centre – and it would be theirs. They'd come to their own Welfare Clinic – out of curiosity and local pride at first, and then because they were really getting something out of it. Look at the women with their Farm Club! They created it and they come to it! Those women would be thrilled at having their own maternity centre.'

'Maybe,' Sue agreed. 'But we haven't got a hospital and I've got five villages. I can't even swing a weekly Mothers' Club, except in Springdale. The women in the other villages haven't time, in fact, to come away over there. I know they go to the Farm Club – but there's a branch in each village and it meets once a month. I can't have five weekly Mothers' Clubs in five different places! Not without a high-powered plane, I can't!'

It was at this point that Marianna quietly gathered up her books and went upstairs, an expression of extreme boredom on her face.

Sue and Bill exchanged a despairing glance.

'Never mind,' Bill said. 'Wait until June, when she starts going out with you. Have you asked her if she'd like to go?'

'Yes – and she said she supposed she might as well do that as anything else.'

Marianna was no more amenable in June than she had been in May. The forested mountains dreaming in blue haze had no charms for anyone whose mind dwelt on New York's skyline. The roar of mountain streams and the water smoke that hung over them were as nothing to the sound of the underground and the smell of carbon monoxide.

School was done on the twentieth of June, and Marianna began her trips with Sue around the country, gloomily, holding the cheerful Maxl in her lap.

Sue's first move was to take her to Harville in an effort to make her realize some of the broader aspects of nursing. Here, she thought, was a perfect example in miniature of the things that Public Health nurses were trying to change – wretched housing, wrong food, ignorance, appalling sanitation, defective children. Marianna was impresssd, but not as Sue had hoped.

'You ain't gettin' nowhere with 'em,' Marianna said. 'They think you're swell but they don't do nothin' about it. What's th' use?'

Sue tried to explain. 'These things take a very long time, Marianna. All I can hope to accomplish this year is some improvement in the children. Miss Mowbray's going to see that they're sent to the Child Welfare Conference, and I'm trying to teach the mothers something about child training and diets. It may seem discouraging to you but it doesn't to me. Do you realize that the Child Welfare Conferences in this State, in one year, have examined and treated *effectively* over five thousand defective children?'

Marianna shrugged.

Sue assured herself that this, too, would take time. She didn't believe she was making a mistake in trying to persuade Marianna to go into nursing. It wasn't as if Marianna wanted to do something else equally worth while. She mustn't go back to New York's slums, and there was no reason why she shouldn't make a good nurse. She was capable and intelligent. Her speech and her lack of education could be remedied. A nurse's training would teach her self-discipline. Her unresponsiveness to people was most certainly due to shyness and a feeling of social inadequacy, rather than to an absence of sympathy. All that was needed was a renewal of Marianna's desire to become a nurse, and somehow this must be accomplished.

It was in June, too, that Bill's brother came back from Europe. Bill had only the meagre lodging in Springdale, and a place must be found for Eliot near Boston, where he could have daily electrical treatments.

Bill was gone a week and it was during his absence that Sue and Marianna had their experience with the raft. A request for a doctor had been relayed from a cabin far back in the hills, where someone was reported to have a broken leg. Sue tried to get in touch with old Dr. Vinal, who was to be called in Bill's place if emergencies arose. Dr. Vinal couldn't be found, and Sue realized that she must go herself and do what she could.

She collected bandages and a variety of splints from Bill's surgery, and then, accompanied by Marianna and Maxl, set out on the long drive. Roads were soupy with mud, streams were overrunning their banks, and the location of the cabin was uncertain. It was mid-afternoon by the time a farmer directed them to a wagon road, which wandered into a wooded valley.

'Ye'll hev to leave th' car here,' he warned Sue. 'There's a pond back in there, just afore ye git to Martin's cabin, an' it's over its banks some.'

'How far is the cabin?'

'About a mile, shouldn't wonder.'

The girls left the reproachful Maxl in the car and continued on foot, Sue carrying her bag and Marianna the splints and bandages.

'This ain't no mile,' Marianna said after a time. 'It's eighty city blocks, I'll betcha.'

'I could bear that,' said Sue, 'but look ahead! He said the pond was over its banks *some*!'

The pond was no longer a pond. It was an extensive shallow lake – into which their road disappeared with disconcerting finality.

Sue halted, to stare across the shimmering expanse. 'That must be the cabin – over there on the hillside. But how do we get across?'

'Ain't that a thing?' Marianna pointed to a log raft tilted against the partly submerged root of a pine tree.

'A thing's the right word for it! But it'll have to do – unless we can make somebody hear, and come and get us. We'd better try a couple of good yells.'

They shrieked in unison, their voices echoing across the water, and the sound brought a tiny figure to the door of the cabin. The figure waved helplessly.

'Come on,' said Sue. 'We'll have to do it on our own. If you'll hold the things I'll pole the raft – if it's got a pole.'

It had a pole.

The girls pushed the unwieldy float off the root and scrambled aboard. The raft moved forward sluggishly, resisting Sue's efforts with the pole, and she perceived that it was dragging slightly on the bottom. It made progress, however, and was a good three-quarters of the way across the shallow water when, without the slightest warning, it began quietly to sink.

'Yowser!' Marianna gasped.

'Hold those bandages high – and my bag!' Sue ordered.

Marianna obeyed automatically, her eyes shining with excitement.

The raft settled deeper and the water rose to the girls' knees – to their waists. It was very cold water. But it ceased to rise above their waists, and after a moment Sue realized what had happened – the logs had gone deep enough for the water to take some of the girls' weight. The raft could carry the rest – even if it did so several feet under.

'There must have been a sudden drop in the ground,' Sue

thought. 'We were touching bottom all the way, until now.' She turned to look at the grinning Marianna, who was sturdily holding bag, splints, and bandages against her chest, the water lapping round her waist.

'How ya doin'?' Marianna inquired cheerfully.

'I'm not doing. But maybe I'd better. Hold steady now.' She propelled the raft forward gingerly under water until a slight jar told her she had reached a shallower spot. She peered down towards the bottom. 'We can wade the rest of the way,' she announced.

'Okay.'

They stepped forward off the front end of the raft and waded ashore – the raft walloping behind them – and confronted a thin, stoop-shouldered woman in a faded overall.

'My land!' she wailed. 'What in *tunket* possessed ye to tackle that old raft? Why didn't ye come th' back road?'

'Back road?' said Sue and Marianna together.

'Sartin'. There 'tis – behind th' house! I didn't take in what ye was a doin', over there, till ye got started. That raft wun't hold nothin'. It's one my boys built when they was the raft age, and it's been a kickin' round th' pond ever since. Land! Ye do be wet! Come along in th' house an' dry your –'

The dripping, shivering Sue interrupted. 'Are you Mrs. Martin? Is your husband here?'

'I be, an' he ain't.'

'Well, I'm the Visiting Nurse. We got your message and came as soon as we could. They said someone here had a broken leg, and the doctor was out –' She paused, arrested by an extraordinary expression on the woman's lined face.

'I – I'm dretful sorry, Nurse. I – we – 'twas th' *cow*! She cut her leg on th' fence. We wanted a vet. I – dunno who could a called ye – one th' neighbours, likely, or –'

At this point Marianna, dripping among the tree stumps, burst into shouts of laughter, and after a dazed second Sue and Mrs. Martin joined her.

'Land!' Mrs. Martin gasped, at last. 'I guess we're crazy –

all of us – a cacklin' here, with you two soppin' wet! You come right along with me!'

The girls followed her, spattering and squelching, into the neat cabin – to the warmth of fire and the comfort of hot coffee.

Later a passing neighbour of the Martins took them back round the pond in his car by another road, and deposited them, dry and grateful, beside their own car – where the frantic Maxl forgave them for everything.

'Whoopee!' said Marianna, as Sue's engine began to purr. 'I ain't had so much fun since I left N' York! But what a life! B'lieve me – I wouldn't be a nurse! Darn near drowned yourself for an old cow.'

Sue ignored this. 'You were a darned good sport, Marianna,' she said.

'You're pretty swell to do things with, yourself.'

Sue reported this conversation to Veazie Ann, later that night. 'Marianna really had a marvellous time – but she still doesn't get the point about nursing.'

Veazie Ann nodded. 'I'll tell ye what 'tis. She don't take no stock in what you're tryin' to do for folks in general because it ain't real to her. What she wants is sumpthin' she can git a holt of – excitement – somethin' happ'nin', high, wide, an' handsome.'

'But goodness, Veazie Ann, I can't go round whanging people with axes or running over them just to give Marianna a concrete demonstration of the kind of nursing that might appeal to her!'

'I know. It's kinder tough to git her to see th' forest instead of th' trees. I guess it's because she's young – an' she's had to look after herself.' Veazie Ann's rocking chair creaked in the brief silence. 'Ye know what,' the calm voice went on again, 'it ain't so much fun, bein' young. I can remember how 'twas. It's kinder like wakin' up slow out of a dream. There don't nothin' seem real but what touches ye. 'Tain't selfishness, like some think – anyway, not how *they* mean. It's just not bein' able to hitch up to things.'

'Yes!' said Sue, startled. 'That's exactly it! I remember too. And people keep expectin' you to take hold, and you can't seem to, and it sort of scares you. You think maybe you're a bad person – but you don't *feel* that you're bad – and you get mixed up, and defiant. But when something very dramatic happens it *does* wake you up, so that for just a minute you feel a part of things. I ought to be more patient with Marianna.'

'You're doin' all right, Sue. But if ye get a chance to let her see some doin's – ye better.'

'I will,' Sue promised.

'Doin's,' however, seemed very scarce. There was nothing, during July, except routine work, thunderstorms, and the fact that Bill was getting a lively, lucrative, and extremely boring practice from among the summer camps and hotels. There was also an influx of doctors who, Bill complained, would vanish in the autumn, leaving him with work enough for ten.

'All the same,' he remarked to Sue one afternoon when they drove past the lovely old house which was to have been theirs, 'if this keeps up maybe our wedding won't be as far off as we'd feared. How would you like that?'

'What do you think?'

'More than I'm going to tell you just now, my sweet.'

Towards the end of July Sue encountered Elias Todd on the street in Springdale, and he paused to speak to her and to Maxl. He was more cordial than he had been at their one previous meeting and he seemed greatly pleased with Maxl's general fitness. Lot Phinney, sitting on the Post Office steps, snorted audibly as he watched the portly Elias grow purple in the face from stooping over Maxl.

Lot's only comment on Maxl had been made months before – shortly after the puppy's arrival.

'Humph!' he said, peering at Maxl. 'Looks like a snake! Wouldn't have th' thing in th' house 'f 'twas me!'

Marianna had been furious. 'The old fool!' she spluttered. '*Snake!*'

But Sue only laughed.

Marianna was still going out faithfully with Sue, day after day, getting up early, going to Bill's surgery while Sue collected her day's list of calls, riding with her from village to village, attending the Mothers' Club meetings in Springdale, and helping to get children off to camps.

'It's the bunk!' Marianna said from time to time. 'Tellin' people to eat their spinach, an' here, drink this, an' don't let Willie stick th' baby with the bread knife.'

'But anything has its dull aspects,' Sue protested – uselessly, she knew.

Meanwhile the lovely August days were melting away, and when the one really dramatic thing happened which might have changed Marianna's mind, she was at the cinema, and did not know of it until she returned home.

That was the Saturday night that Bill, operating on a kitchen table, removed Ira Prouty's appendix. Sue had assisted, and Kit, in Springdale for the week-end as usual, had acted as anaesthetist. But hearing about a thing second-hand, when it is all over, is not very effective. Marianna had not been greatly impressed. She was far more excited by having seen the Winslow Hospital ambulance taking one of the guests from Bald Trail Inn through the village on the way to Winslow. Elias Todd had followed the ambulance in his own car, and Marianna was able to relate, at home, that everyone said the guest hadn't wanted to go to Winslow. He had wanted to have his attack of influenza and pneumonia where he was, and not be dragged fifty miles over mountain roads. It was rumoured that the man had threatened to sue Elias if the trip to Winslow had any ill-effects, and Elias had had to agree to pay the hospital expenses before the man would be removed.

Bill, who had been called in on the case, confirmed most of this. The man was quite able to be moved, he said, but it would be very unfortunate for Elias if anything *did* go wrong. There'd be a lot of unpleasant publicity, if nothing else.

During August, Sue and Kit attacked Marianna's other bugbear – her dislike of the country. Sue had every Saturday afternoon off, and Kit, who had bought a small car, drove over from Winslow at noon. Together they escorted Marianna over every inch of the White Mountains. Sometimes Veazie Ann went with them, and always the perpetually thrilled Maxl, who had now reached the out-at-elbows stage of growth, and seemed all joints and ears. Next to Sue, he adored Marianna, and being devoured with curiosity spent most of the time on these excursions dangling out of the car window while Marianna clung to his tail. His long nose bored into the wind, his ears streamed back, turning up brown undersides, his short, pipestem hind legs kept up a continual trampling on Marianna's lap.

'He has an awful good time, don't he?' she said once. 'You know, I never had nothin' to do with dogs before. He – don't seem like an animal at all. He's more like a person.'

'All dogs are like that when you get to know them,' said Sue, hoping that if all else failed Marianna might stay because she couldn't bear to leave Maxl. The hope was a slim one, but still – it was a possibility.

Bill was too busy these days to accompany the girls, but he made an excellent suggestion.

'The kid's romantic at heart,' he said. 'Fill her up with the legends of the White Mountains. Veazie Ann knows 'em. She'll help you.'

'But isn't Marianna going to smell a rat? If she thinks we're doing this on purpose it won't work.'

'It will if Kit's the one who wants to know about everything. After all, here's a nice Canadian girl who ought to be enlightened about the charms of New England. What more do you need?'

So it was to Kit that the stories were told, and Kit asked questions so skilfully that the entire history of the White Mountains was poured into Marianna's ears.

The girls went, first of all, to Mount Washington, and rode to the summit on the cog railway. They saw the pile of rocks marking the spot where the unfortunate Miss Bourne had died of exhaustion in one of the early ascents of the mountain.

They heard about the terrific winds, the paralysing frost clouds, they saw the alpine plants which grew nowhere else south of the Arctic Circle – tea plant, bearberry, heath, saxifrage, arctic rushes. They saw the icy mountain lakes and looked down upon the fat backs of clouds.

They went to the Notches – Dixville, Pinkham, Franconia – and Veazie Ann related the legend of the Great Carbuncle supposed to have been hidden in a cave by the Indians – a vast stone, so brilliant that it lighted all the hills around by night and could sometimes be seen scintillating by day. Whoever glimpsed its rays was struck by a peculiar madness and ever after wandered through the gorges in search of it.

They went to Lost River and saw the spot where the river vanishes underground. They saw Echo Lake, and the Flume, and the Old Man of the Mountains – that giant stone face believed by the Indians to be guardian of the 'Crystal Hills'.

'He's calmed down some, now,' Veazie Ann said. 'But in them days he was pretty bumptious – a flashin' fire from his eyes, an' a turnin' to stone folks that tried to git through the passes.'

Marianna sniffed at this, but she was interested, the girls knew.

The mountains reared great shaggy heads into the clouds. Cool winds blew through gorges sweet with the smell of pines and noisy with the voices of waterfalls. Cannon Mountain's aerial tramway took the girls high up into the pure, clear air and they looked across a hundred miles of blue peaks, and down upon silver lakes, and blue threads that were rivers, and pine forests that seemed no more than an inch in height – green rugs on the knees of the mountains.

'If Marianna doesn't fall for this,' Sue thought, 'she's crazy.' Certainly Marianna was having a good time. She was tanned, and clear-eyed, and hard-muscled, and she was in high spirits – though whether because she was enjoying herself, or because the time was approaching when she would leave, they did not know.

T—F

In September the leaves began to turn and the hills flamed. School opened the Monday after Labour Day, but Marianna continued to ride round the country with Sue, and Veazie Ann reported that she was 'a sortin' of her clothes and fixin' to pack'.

'Oh, golly!' Sue wailed. 'Do you suppose *none* of this has done any good? I – I've thought lately that she was a little bit interested in what I've been doing.'

'She said anything?'

'Only that I'm wasting my time because the minute I relax my supervision they'll all be back where they were. How *can* she think that, Veazie Ann?'

'She don't – really. I'm sartin she's kinder impressed – only she ain't impressed enough to stay.'

'I suppose so. Oh, if only *something* would happen!'

And something did, though it was scarcely what Sue had in mind.

18

Marianna assists

IT began with a spell of rainy weather, in the midst of which Kit telephoned from Winslow.

'I can't have the week-end,' she began. 'Miss Tripp wants it. So I'm taking my afternoon off today – and I'll have all tomorrow. I thought I'd come over.'

'Oh, golly! I'll be working!'

'That's all right. The weather's so ghastly I'll just sleep.'

She arrived late that afternoon, just as Sue and Marianna were getting home, and after dinner Bill appeared, with the news that Florida was due for a hurricane, and that storm warnings were posted all along the coast.

'That means we'll get some high winds around here tomorrow,' he said. 'And last time Florida had a hurricane *we* had a lot of branches strewn over the roads. You'd better be careful, darling. Do you have to go very far out into the country tomorrow?'

'Only on the Pow case,' said Sue. 'We'll be back by eleven.'

'That's all right then.' Bill was relieved. 'It won't start to blow here until afternoon.'

Sue wasn't worrying about winds – she was too busy. But the sky did look unpleasant the next morning, with heavy, dark clouds scudding over the mountains and the rain falling steadily.

'Would you rather stay at home today?' she asked Marianna at breakfast.

'Gosh, no! There ain't nothin' to do. Kit'll sleep till noon.'

Sue's case was about ten miles from Springdale – not much of a drive if the road hadn't been narrow, winding, and steep. The air was heavy, too, and Sue drove in a bleak silence, feeling oddly depressed. Maxl shivered in his coat and refused to sit in Marianna's lap – insisting on lying as close to Sue as possible.

'What's the matter with him?' Marianna demanded, hurt.

'I don't know. He acts frightened, doesn't he?'

She reached down to pat the little dog. 'It's all right, Maxl,' she said.

He caught the steady reassurance in her voice and relaxed, tail quivering briefly. Then his eyes closed and he slept.

Sue's patient was a young farmer who had fallen from a load of hay early in the summer, injuring his back. He was recovering slowly, but he still required a good deal of nursing and most of this his wife was unable to do since she was expecting a baby at any moment. Sue managed to pay a visit to the farm at least every other day, and the case was one which Marianna used as a typical example in her insistence upon the general dullness of nursing.

'Sure you help 'em,' she said. 'But if you wasn't around one of the neigbours would come in.'

'But the nearest neighbour is two miles away. Do you really think, after everything you've seen this summer, that all this is pointless?'

'No,' said Marianna honestly after a pause. 'I guess it ain't; but I think you do an awful lot of hard work an' an awful lot of dull work. I know you do it better than somebody that wasn't trained, but it – it just don't seem *worth it*, to me.'

Sue would have been encouraged by Marianna's admission that the summer's experience had not been entirely wasted if it hadn't been for the fact that October was almost upon them. There was no time to press the advantage of this slightly broadened viewpoint.

When they reached the farm, Maxl, who ordinarily was content to remain in the car, or at any rate was resigned to being left, made un unexpected and frenzied protest. He scrabbled at Sue with his paws, and pleaded, wild-eyed, to be taken along.

A faint, distant roll of thunder explained this. Maxl was terrified in thunderstorms.

'He musta been hearing it even when we couldn't,' Marianna said. 'Want me to stay with him?'

But Maxl would have none of that. He wanted to be in a house, where there were nice dark corners. He wanted to be with Sue. He wanted something decidedly different from what he had.

'Never mind,' said Sue, laughing. 'We'll take him inside. It's not a strictly professional thing to do, but it doesn't matter in this case, and the Pows won't care. Take him in the kitchen, Marianna. Maybe that'll calm him down.'

Marianna settled herself in the big kitchen with Maxl and young Mrs. Pow, while Sue retired to the bedroom to give the strenuous massage which was her chief reason for coming. Mrs. Pow had spread a table with newspapers for Sue's bag. There were soap and hot water ready, and a paper bag for waste. Alf Pow had been combed and brushed, and made neat with a clean nightshirt.

Sue was gratified, as always. She had only had to explain this once to Mrs. Pow, and ever since had found things done exactly right.

'Your wife's a born nurse,' she said to Alf, as she removed her cuffs and rolled up her sleeves.

'Yup. She ain't bad,' said Alf, bursting with pride.

Sue opened her bag, greased her hands with cocoa butter, and set to work. She could hear the murmur of voices in the kitchen and the nervous click of Maxl's claws on the floor. Outside, occasional gusts of wind drove hard spears of rain against the windows.

The massage was nearly done when the bedroom door opened abruptly and Marianna, very white, beckoned to Sue. She said nothing whatever, but the appeal in her eyes was so urgent that Sue hurried across to her.

'What's the matter?'

'M-Mrs. Pow says the baby's coming – right now!'

'Heavens!' Sue turned to Alf and explained, her voice calm, her expression reassuring.

Alf was startled but not alarmed. 'Go ahead. I'm all right. 'Twun't take long, Miss Barton. She's built like her mother, an' *she* had her babies awful quick.'

He couldn't have said anything more alarming to Sue. If this was to be a rapid birth there would be no time to get Bill – *or* to do anything except stand by. There was no telephone in the house. Marianna couldn't drive – and anyway, Sue would need help.

'I'm in for it this time,' she thought, and dashed out to the kitchen, Marianna close behind.

An examination of Mrs. Pow told Sue that the baby was indeed coming – and at once.

'Why didn't you tell me?' she asked.

'I didn't know, Miss Barton. It begun all at once – just like Ma. I thought it would be next week; but I got everything ready, like you told me – th' oilcloth for the bed an' th' extra sheet – th' bed's all made up in th' spare room.' Mrs. Pow was as unruffled as her husband had been. 'You want I should go to bed right off?' she added.

'Yes. Marianna, go with her.'

Left alone, Sue put Maxl on top of a china cupboard, where he would be out of the way, and started a large kettle of water boiling.

'Mrs. Pow,' she called. 'Did you sterilize the towels and pads and things?'

'Yes, I did, Miss Barton – in the pillowcase like you said – an' dried 'em in the oven. They're here in th' cupboard.'

Sue breathed a blessing on the intelligent Mrs. Pow, and went for her instrument case. 'Let's see,' she thought. 'I've got everything except the pails of water. Marianna can do that.'

Sue's own little enamel pan would do for sterilizing her scissors and forceps. She put them on to boil, scrubbed her hands, and hurried to the spare room.

'Marianna,' she ordered. 'I want two pails of water in here –

one of them cold, the other hot, but not too hot. There's water on boiling. When I tell you, fill the second pail and add cold until the temperature's 115°. There's a bath thermometer in my bag.'

Marianna went, without a word. There was no objection now, Sue noted, to taking orders.

A seven-and-a-half-pound boy was born in exactly one hour, with very little trouble for his mother. The trouble began after his birth – and for Sue.

The baby didn't breathe.

Sue held him by the feet, head down, and slapped him. Nothing happened. She plunged him into cold and then hot water. He still didn't breathe, and he was turning blue.

'Blanket!' Sue ordered.

Marianna leapt.

They carried the motionless baby to the kitchen and put him on the table, where Sue tried artificial respiration – to no avail.

'W-what is it?' Marianna quavered. 'Is – is he gonna die?'

'I don't know.' Sue tried to clear the mucus from the little throat with a piece of gauze wrapped round her finger. The baby continued to lie motionless. There was one last chance. Sue laid a thin piece of gauze over the baby's mouth, put her own young lips upon it, and sucked – with all her strength.

The kitchen clock ticked loudly in the silence and outside the wind rose in a sudden howl. Maxl whimpered, a small frightened sound – or was it Maxl?

The baby's fists stirred against Sue's throat, and she straightened up quickly. There was a gurgling squawk and then a long-drawn lusty bellow as life-giving air rushed into new lungs.

Sue grinned into Marianna's tearful eyes.

'There he goes!' she said.

'B-but what was it?'

'Mucus in his throat.'

'An' – an' you got it out – like that?'

'Well, I certainly didn't get it out by singing to him.'

'Will he live?'

'Look at him! And listen to him!'

The baby was now red and squirming, and his yells rose above the sound of the storm.

'G-geeze!' Marianna gasped.

'Well, come on! We've got plenty more to do! You run and tell Alf he has a son. I'll see to Mrs. Pow – and this young man.'

It was noon before they left the house, and then they had to stop at the neighbour's farm to send someone to take care of the mother and baby.

They went back to Springdale through blinding rain and rocking gusts of wind that bent the trees almost to the ground. Sue was too busy keeping the car on the road to do any wondering about Marianna, and neither of the girls spoke, except to make startled comments on the storm, or comfort the terrified Maxl.

19

A day and a night

SPRINGDALE'S Main Street was noise and water and dimness, the houses lurid in a greenish-yellow light. Elms strained lashing arms towards the earth, and the car passed trembling beneath them. A shutter flew by and crashed into a store window. A well bucket dragging a long chain rolled out of a driveway and fled down the street. Where the mountains had been was a piling turmoil of clouds, while through and above everything ran the high shuddering scream of the wind.

'Geeze!' Marianna shouted. 'I never seen nothin' like this! What is it?'

'Neither have I. I don't know!' Sue yelled.

A blurred figure in yellow oilskins appeared suddenly before them. It waved frantically, leaning against the wind as against a wall.

Sue's foot came down on the brake. The figure sprang to the rear door of the car, tore it open, and leapt inside, panting.

It was Freddie Bowker, a tall, gangling high-school senior, cousin to the Jim Bowker who drove the milk lorry.

The boy was pale with exertion. He had lost his hat, and his tow-coloured hair streamed water. He wiped at his face with a shaky hand.

'Golly, Miss Barton!' he gasped, ignoring Marianna. 'I – I thought you'd never – get here! Doc Barry says – come to the church right – off!'

'The *church*! What's happened?'

Freddie grinned wanly. 'Look out the winder,' he said, 'an you'll see it happenin'! That there breeze is the Florida hurricane.'

'*Hurricane!*'

'Yup! And the dam's giving way up at the lake. Everybody's at the church. Soon's you get up the hill outer the wind I'll tell you.'

Sue swung the car to the right, along the road that led out of that end of the valley and up to the rocky promontory high above town, where the Congregational Church, pastorless at the moment, looked down on the roofs of Main Street. The road up, sheltered by the mountain, was clear of debris, and the drums of the wind grew high and far away. Sue's headlights were on, but she could see only a few feet ahead of the car and the curtain of rain advanced with it. But here, at least, one could speak without yelling. As Freddie's breathing grew easier he began to talk.

Sue listened, struggling with the car. Marianna stroked the jittery Maxl and said nothing with her most contemptuous city air, though Freddie's story, as Marianna admitted afterwards, was certainly something!

The three days of rain had swollen the lake until, with this morning's cloudburst, the dam had begun to weaken, and since noon everyone had known that it would go. If it gave all at once every house in Springdale would be swept from its foundations, and Lot Phinney had said there was only one thing to do – the sluice gates must be opened and the lake let into the valley slowly instead of in one great wall of water. There were twenty men at the dam, working to reinforce it – to make it hold until everyone was out of the valley. They were waiting as long as they dared, but when the centre of the dam began to bulge they must open the gates. All the people of Springdale who lived on the floor of the valley had left, and as many as possible had taken refuge in houses which were above the valley. The rest were in the church – about two hundred of them, especially those who had been injured by falling trees, stones, or timbers. Dr. Barry had said that the sick or injured should be in one place, where he could tend them. Freddie, and now Marianna, would be the only high-school students at the church, for all the others had gone to the homes of friends.

The uninjured men at the church would sleep in Smalley's big barn farther up the hill, to make extra room for women, children, and the injured. Mrs. Cooney had come to help the doctor, and Mrs. Edgett, in the village when word came about the dam, was now at the church helping Mrs. Cooney.

'Doc Barry's been swell!' Freddie said, glowing with hero worship. 'It was him said get to the church, on account of it was the one safe place with a furnace. He had 'em taking lorry-loads of canned food up from Fogg's store, and the church dishes from the town hall, an' the kerosene stove. And he took all the medicine and things from his surgery, and he sent up to Bald Trail Inn and told Elias Todd to give us all the blankets he had. Todd done it, too, and come himself to see the blankets was took care of, and by golly' – Freddie slapped his wet knee – 'the old coot can't get back now. Martha Edgett grappled on to him and she's been working him like a dog, helping get folks dried and fed. Last I seen before I came away, he was climbing down the hill from Smalley's, lugging two big buckets of water. Boy! I'll betcha he ain't lifted anything heavier 'n a handkerchief in twenty years! He –'

'Wait a minute, Freddie,' Sue interrupted. 'What were *you* doing down in the valley?'

'Looking for you,' the boy said simply.

'All alone?' said Sue, aghast. What were they thinking of to send a boy out under such circumstances?'

'Somebody had to come,' Freddie said. 'Doc asked for a volunteer to stop your car when you came into town. He said whoever went was to wait an hour, and then, if you didn't come, to get back to the church and he'd go down himself. I didn't wait for anybody to stop me. I ran for the door and hollered back that I was gone. He couldn't do anything about it. After all, I'm an Eagle Scout. Besides, there ain't any danger yet. Wun't be for a while, they think.'

The church was just over the rise now, a ponderous, misty whiteness through the downpour. The car ground towards it in low gear.

'Thank you very much, Freddie,' said Sue, and smiled at him over her shoulder.

'Aw, 'twarn't nothin',' said Freddie, dazzled.

'Did you walk down?'

'Dunno's you'd call it that. I just kinder spread out like a glider and come down on the wind. 'Twarn't any slow motion, b'lieve me.' Freddie grinned. 'I thought it was a good chance to get some practice before I go to flying school.'

Marianna turned her head and spoke for the first time. '*You* gonna be a pilot?'

'Yup.' Freddie's eyes were hostile, and Marianna's, which had been eager for an instant, hardened in return.

'Look!' said Sue hastily into the icy silence. 'People have saved their cats and dogs. See! In the cars around the church!'

'Geeze!' Marianna said, as Sue manoeuvred into a space among the ranks of cars at the back of the church. 'Lookit all their little faces lookin' outa th' car windows!'

'I hate girls that swear!' said Freddie briefly.

'An' I hate Eagle Scouts!'

Sue switched off the engine. 'Come on, kids,' she said pacifically. 'Leave Maxl, Marianna. He'll be all right for now. They can't have animals underfoot inside.'

They stepped out into the downpour and dashed across the churchyard to the back entry, the wind, even in this sheltered spot, rocking them on their feet.

A babble of voices met Sue as she opened the door – voices and warmth and the mingled smells of soup, wet clothing, and musty pews.

Freddie's mother, wild-eyed, hurried down the aisle to put a trembling hand on the boy's sleeve. 'You ought to git a lickin' – big 's ye be,' she faltered.

Freddie touched the worn hand with an awkward boy's finger.

'Now, Ma!' he said gently, and glared at Marianna, who laughed and turned away.

The pews were crowded – except those doing duty as sick-beds. Voices murmured, heads bobbed, damp figures stood in little groups. Children pattered in the aisles. In one corner was a vast mountain of blankets; in another a kerosene stove was partly concealed by the movements of Veazie Ann and Martha Edgett. Elias Todd, red-faced and minus his necktie, was struggling with a heavy iron kettle.

'*Here she is!*' Ira Prouty sang out from where he was sitting on the chancel steps. Heads turned as though pulled by one string. 'Miss Barton's safe! Freddie's back! Hey, Miss Barton Did ja know you're the last one up?' Veazie Ann and Martha Edgett turned in sudden gladness, and the garish light from the big kerosene-burning chandelier shone on resigned faces that broke into smiles now, greeting their lost Visiting Nurse.

Sue laughed and waved and nodded, but her eyes were sweeping the church for Bill's dark head, for his lean clear-cut face, for some familiar gesture. He wasn't anywhere!

The giant hand of the wind tolled the church bell over her head.

'Sue!' It was Kit's voice from the front vestibule doorway. She was beckoning.

Sue's progress along the side aisle was slowed by battered townspeople crowding to speak to her, to tell her how worried they had been, how glad they were, now that she was safe. Most of them were wet; many were bruised and limping. But Sue had almost been given up for lost, when everyone else was safe – and they forgot their discomfort in their relief.

'And I didn't even know it was a hurricane, so I wasn't scared,' she told them, and they marvelled, forgetting that they, too, had not been alarmed until the word 'hurricane' had come to them over radios now dead.

Sue reached Kit at last and was drawn out into the vestibule, where a table was stacked with bandages, splints, ointments, and antiseptics.

'He's *all right!*' Kit said. 'Don't look like that! He just went up to Smalley's barn with Lot Phinney to make sure everything would be dry for the men to sleep there tonight. He was going down to the valley in a few minutes to – to – wait until you came – if you *di* – oh, for heaven's sake, Bat, go and wash your face! It looks as if you'd been nuzzling in mud!' Her arm was light around Sue's shoulders for an instant.

Sue made a small face at her. 'What's to be done here, Kit?'

'A lot. Nobody's seriously injured, but a good many have been hit by falling debris – stones and bricks and branches. We've got a broken hand – jammed in a car door – but Bill's fixed that. There are six cut heads, three sprained ankles, got dashing back into houses for things at the last minute, one greenstick fracture of the collarbone, got by being slammed against a telephone pole by the wind, and Tom Ventress, who was hit by a falling rock at the dam. He's in the front pew, unconscious.'

'Fractured skull?'

'No, just stunned. But everybody else can hobble around. Bill thought the best thing to do was to set up this table out here and do the dressings. I was just going to start.'

'Golly, Kit! What a wretched business! When are they going to let the lake in?'

'Nobody knows exactly. Not until they have to, I suppose. It doesn't matter so much now. Everybody's safe. Sue – there's Bill.'

He had come in quietly and was bending over the pew that held the unconscious Tom Ventress. Sue took an impulsive step forward across the vestibule threshold, her hair aflame against the white walls behind her. The movement caught Bill's attention and their eyes met in a single clear look.

Then Bill lifted one hand in a half-salute and Sue smiled. That was all. But the memory of that look wrapped Sue in a warmth of security through all the hours that followed.

They went to work at once. Kit collected the injured into the rear pews and called them out two at a time. Bill examined the injuries, gave his brief orders, and the girls carried them out, working silently. Marianna was posted with a cup and whisky, doling it out, as requested by Bill, to those who were wet, exhausted, or faint. Freddie, fascinated in the doorway, was sent by Bill to settle the bandaged in pews on either side of the centre aisle, where they would be unitedly accessible; to fold coats for pillows; to wrap drenched people in blankets. Veazie Ann and Martha Edgett ladled hot soup into thick white bowls and sent it round by Elias Todd – who seemed to be the only thoroughly dry person in the place.

Mr. Todd seemed a little astonished at finding himself in the rôle of waiter, but Martha Edgett gave him no time to reflect. 'We're about th' only ones that ain't in a state of mind or body,' she said crisply, 'so we'll leave the others be. Here's two more, Mr. Todd. Hurry now. An' don't spill it! We got none to waste!' Mrs. Edgett was enjoying herself.

The last cut head was just emerging from the vestibule when Lot Phinney noticed that the wind had stopped.

'It'll begin again,' Bill said, 'as soon as the centre of the storm has passed over – and it'll come from the other direction. We'll get the worst of it *here*, then.' He stepped to the door. 'Freddie! This is a good time to take water to the animals in the cars!'

'Yessir!'

'And you might keep an eye on the rear doors. Don't let any of the children go wandering out.'

'Yes, *sir*!'

Sue had little chance for conversation with Bill, and their few exchanges of words were impersonal. She told him about the Pow baby, and once they spoke of the animals outside. Bill told her that cattle, horses, and pigs had been driven up the hillsides, out of reach of the coming flood, and left to shift for themselves. They would be all right if they didn't try to go back down.

'What about feeding the animals in the cars?'

'I'm afraid we can't, tonight. We've got about a hundred and eighty people in here to be fed, and I had no time to count stores or make plans. Also, I don't know whether we'll be able to get out of here tomorrow. I should think we would. At least, everybody who can move under his own power ought to be able to get out. And there are plenty of farms to take people in. But the sick and the old will have to stay here until the roads are cleared – so I don't dare be lavish with the stores. The animals will be all right for a bit if they have water, and tomorrow they can be let out – most of them.'

The ominous quiet outside the church continued, the only sound being a light patter of rain. The air was warmer, too, as Sue discovered when she stepped to the front door for a breath of fresh air. Ira Prouty had preceded her and was standing at the bottom of the broad white steps. He was still pale from his operation, she noted, and he was bent forward looking down into the valley. He didn't hear her on the steps above him.

'Hey!' he shouted, turning. '*It's a comin'!*'

His voice carried back into the church through the open door and there was hurried tramping inside as people crowded to the windows or hurried out to the steps.

Twilight had not yet fallen and in the calm central eye of the hurricane everything was clear. The white-faced watchers in the church, staring down, saw a boiling white surge sweep down their little river, saw the river leave its banks and spread, gleaming silver in the fading light. Silently, through the minutes, they watched that shining expanse creep up Main Street, where they had always parked their cars. It flowed over their neat lawns among their lilac bushes; it crept on to the porches where they sat on summer evenings.

And then, from high overhead, the wind charged again, and the heavens opened.

'Get back inside!' Bill shouted. 'Everybody back in!'

They obeyed him without a word, filing decorously through the open doors – to the sudden tolling of the bell by that terrible unseen hand – and the doors closed behind them, shutting them into the groaning, cracking church – shutting out the darkness, the sledge hammers of the rain, the renewed terror of the wind. And they went, from instinct and long habit, to their family pews, and sat down quietly, waiting, not needing to watch to know what was happening below.

The water would be creeping up to the ground-floor windows, pouring in, staining their Nottingham-lace curtains, flooding the Brussels carpets in their parlours, lapping on their front stairs, floating their dining-room tables, drowning their hard-earned radios. It would surge into their pleasant kitchens, into their stoves, their pickle jars, their flour barrels. It would ripple up the slopes to their barns, splashing under the rain. It would gleam on their threshing floors, pour into the bins of fodder stored for the cattle. Smoke-houses and pig-pens would float away on the current or catch on the corners of porch roofs. Muddy lake water would seep into their upstairs rooms. Feather beds would soak in it, and wedding sheets and towels, and hand-made quilts. It might even reach the attics and have a scum of dust upon it as it washed among old trunks, forgotten saddles, and kegs of beans. But the houses would stand. The houses were good houses and sturdy on strong foundations — built to last, they thought proudly, and turned to one another.

'Well –' they said. And, 'It'll take a little while to clear up the mess, wun't it?'

The bell clamoured over their heads and the chandelier swung on its base as the church rocked, throwing shadows into centre pews among the injured and light into side pews among sleeping children. But the wind was not as violent as it had been, nor as steady.

Sue and Kit went quickly up and down the centre aisle, adjusting bandages, easing cramped positions, bringing drinks of water, heating stones in boiling water for icy feet, settling old ladies. Bill sat with the unconscious Tom Ventress and his fat, silent wife, and Freddie hovered at a respectful distance. Marianna wandered silently about the church and finally sat down in a back pew beside Lot Phinney, who was looking very old and very tired.

Meanwhile, now that the injured and the children had been fed, Veazie Ann and Martha were delving into the stores for corned beef, baked beans, and bread, loading the weary Elias with cans until he staggered. Veazie Ann had brought her largest frying pans and they were put to use heating beans and meat.

The wind was definitely lessening its force now, and the clamour of the church bell faltered, grew thin, and after a while died away. The rain, however, continued.

While supper was in progress, Marianna, who had just received her ration of bread and corned beef, moved unobtrusively to the rear church door and slipped out before Sue could stop her. She returned some ten minutes later, her hair dangling wet round her face, her plate empty and rain-washed in her hand.

Freddie confronted her.

'Did you go out?'

'So what?'

The boy's lips tightened. 'That was a lousy thing to do,' he said clearly.

'Why?'

'The doctor said nobody was to go out. You sneaked.' He stared at the plate. 'What you been doing with that?'

' 'Tain't any of your business – but if you wanta know I took Maxl sump'n to eat. He's out there all alone in Sue's car an' he was hungry.'

'You gave your food to your dog when there are people need it?'

'Aw, fer cryin' out loud! It's my supper, ain't it? I wasn't hungry.'

'You – you mean you're going *without* your supper?'

'I will if I want!' said the furious Marianna.

'Oh,' said Freddie. 'I – I thought –' He was silent, shifting his feet, his eyes embarrassed. 'I – I guess I didn't understand,' he said at last, slowly.

Marianna stared at him, chin high.

'Look,' he said, 'I – I ain't very hungry, neither. You – you could have my supper.'

'Naw!'

The boy flushed. 'Take half, then,' he said. 'Aw, c'mon! I'll — get another plate. We can sit down back. I — I'll *tell you about the flying school*.' He was offering to reveal his dream — his heart's core — to make amends.

It was Marianna's turn to flush. She hesitated.

'Okay,' she said briefly, and Freddie dashed away.

'Lord love a duck!' Kit murmured in Sue's ear. 'Do you see what I see?'

'Mm. Something the hurricane brought along, no doubt.'

'Well, it's high time something brought it — my gosh, Sue! Look what's coming in *now*!'

Sue looked and beheld in the doorway a coated and be-draggled Maxl. His tail drooped and his ears hung to the floor. He dripped.

'Marianna left the door open, I'll bet a dollar!' Sue ex-claimed, and hurried up the aisle. Maxl flung himself upon her, shivering with relief. 'Darling,' Sue told him unhappily, 'I'm afraid you'll have to go straight back. We can't have little dogs in here underfoot.'

'Leave him in, Sue,' Martha Edgett called. 'He wun't do no harm — an' mebbe he'll amuse folks.'

So Maxl stayed, trailing joyfully at Sue's heels, accepting all the attention offered him and snubbing no one. He was very thankful to be inside.

Shortly after this, when the wind was only a breath stirring the trees and the rain had stopped, there was an odd fumbling at the front door. Lot Phinney opened it to admit, one by one, seventeen drenched and stumbling men from the dam. They carried three more on stretchers improvised by tying coats to hastily cut poles. All were dazed from weariness and exposure and they greeted wives and relatives with trembling effort.

'Mr. Todd! Freddie!' Bill ordered. 'Hold a screen of blankets around that stove. Ira, you and Lot get their clothes off and wrap them in blankets. Marianna — whisky! Quarter of a cup each!' He turned to Kit and Sue. 'I'll want you for the stretcher cases! Mrs. Edgett, will you heat blankets at the furnace? Get some of the women to help you. I want *hot* blankets!'

He knelt beside the stretchers on the floor, asking brief questions. A tree had fallen, sweeping the three from the road. The toll was one broken shoulder, one broken leg, one injured back – not broken, Bill said, after an examination, but with badly torn ligaments.

The men's wives stood watching in silent anguish while the girls cut the wet clothing away from broken bones.

'There's no use in my trying to set Ed's leg without X-rays,' Bill said at last. 'I'll splint it and keep him comfortable until he can be taken to Winslow.' He paused. 'I can manage the shoulder. It's a clean break. But we'd better settle George's back, first. He'll have to stay right where he is on the floor for a while.' His hand was gentle on the man's shoulder. 'I'm not going to bother you much until tomorrow, George. But we've got to get these wet things out from under you, and while you're over I'll strap that back.'

'It's all right, Doc,' George whispered. 'It don't hurt much.'

'That's fine! Sue, pull that pole out of the way and hold the coat up against his chest to steady him. Wait a second! Veazie Ann – I want two blankets, folded in half, one inside the other, and roll one edge a third back. Kit! Adhesive! It's in my bag.'

There were rolls of plaster bandage in the bag, too, but Sue and Kit both knew why Bill would not put a cast on the back that night. George's colour was a pale grey, his pulse was slow and weak, and he was covered with a clammy perspiration – all indications of bad shock. He was in no condition to take an anaesthetic of any kind, or to stand the long and, under these circumstances, difficult business of being put in a cast. The only thing, now, was to get him dry and warm, ease the back with temporary strapping, and then keep him quiet.

'Whisky, Marianna!' Bill called, and Marianna sprang away to return with the cup. 'All right now, feller, drink this.'

George drank, his pale lips stiff on the rim of the cup. Then, as a little colour returned to his face, Bill said briefly, 'Ready?'

George nodded. Veazie Ann knelt with the folded blankets. Sue tightened her hold on the coat. 'Shove the edge of the blankets under him when he's turned,' Bill said. 'Now then – easy!' Bill's long fingers closed over his side of the coat that had served as a stretcher; his arms tensed. Slowly, steadily, he lifted, and Sue held fast to her side of the coat. They made a sling of it, one side against George's chest, the other against his back. The limp body came up turning on its side.

'Scissors, Kit!'

George's coat and shirt were cut away. Blankets were tucked against him. Swiftly the clean adhesive was smoothed in overlapping layers on the discoloured back. Bill rolled his side of the stretcher coat into a long loose roll and tucked it along the floor on folded blanket edges. Then, with only his hands for support, he eased George back to the floor. The man was lying now on warm, dry blankets whose folded front edges were on Sue's side, under the roll of coat. She removed the coat and pulled the blankets flat.

'There!' Bill said. 'Now for a pillow of some kind – and lots of hot blankets – and we'll need all the spare coats to pile around him to keep off the draught.'

'Jiminy!' said Ira Prouty, and Elias Todd cleared his throat to comment, 'Very remarkable. Very clever!'

Sue and Kit exchanged amused glances. Bill's best feats of surgery would never, they knew, have been appreciated by his audience, but the simple method of turning George had seemed miraculous – though it was only the method used by every trained nurse in changing a sheet under a helpless patient.

Bill looked up. 'What are you boys doing over here?'

'It's okay, Doc,' Ira said. 'You been a while there. We got everybody in blankets, an' they're all a settin' like a flock of crows.'

The next thing was the shoulder.

'No ether, Doc,' young Ezra said, aware of the circle of faces in general, and of his wife's in particular. 'I can take it!'

The shoulder was simple. One of Bill's hands felt for the break; the other drew the arm forward and up, until the broken bones met, and were bound in place with splints and bandages. It was not permanent, but it would do.

The man stood it without a word. It was Ira Prouty who fainted.

By the time he had been revived, and Ed had been moved to a pew near Tom Ventress, Veazie Ann and Martha Edgett were serving the newcomers hot soup. The men drank it greedily and told their story between gulps.

They got away from the dam without difficulty and had set out on the long climb up the road to the church when the hurricane struck again, hurling trees and boulders, and blowing the men flat to the road. They had struggled on, however, in rain and roaring darkness, making slow progress until Ed and George and Ezra had been hurt by the tree. Then they made no progress at all for a long time – not, in fact, until the wind began to die down and they could carry the injured men, relieving each other every fifteen minutes or so.

'Why didn't you send somebody ahead for help?' Sue asked

'Well, I'll tell ye, Miss Barton. 'T seemed best for us all to keep together an' help each other. There was times when 'twas kinder heavy sleddin'.'

They had simply done their job in the way which seemed most sensible to them. That was all. There was no call to make a fuss.

'Well,' Bill said, and paused.

'Want they should get settled for the night?' Martha Edgett inquired.

'Yes. And the men who are sleeping in Smalley's barn had better go, so that we can have things a little quieter here.'

'All right. I'll tell 'em,' said Mrs. Edgett briskly. 'Mr. Todd, you might pass round them blankets to the folks that's sleepin' here.'

'Certainly, Mrs. Edgett!'

'Give 'em one each.'

'One each,' said Mr. Todd.

Sue watched him trudging up and down the aisles behind a pyramid of blankets. She noticed, as he paused to speak to people, that their greeting was no longer distant, but friendly and casual. Disaster had made him one of them again – for a little.

He was passing Sue, where she stood keeping an eye on George and Tom, when Martha Edgett snapped, 'Mr. Todd, y'd better stay here t'night with us. We're liable to need ye.'

Mr. Todd flushed with pleasure, and catching Sue's eye remarked awkwardly, 'Fine woman, Mrs. Edgett. Seems to know what she's doing!'

'She's splendid,' said Sue warmly, and thought, 'Why, he adores being bossed! He's crazy about it!'

The church grew quiet at last. Bill brought a stepladder from the basement and unscrewed two of the lamps from their places in the chandelier. These would serve as night lights. The others he turned out.

'You girls had better get some sleep,' he said to Sue and Kit as he climbed down.

'Don't be silly!' Kit said. 'You can't be everywhere at once. Suppose Tom Ventress takes a notion to get up and wander around in a daze – just as the old lady Chandler decides to have a heart attack. I'll stay up – but I think Sue ought to get some rest. She's had a hard day.'

Sue protested, but in the end she retired to a remote pew and lay down – with no expectation of falling asleep on that hard ledge. She fell asleep instantly, Maxl curled in a ball against her ankles.

Bill woke her at two o'clock, as he had promised.

'Darling – it's time to get up – if you *will* have it.'

Sue emerged slowly from warm darkness.

'Wh-what?'

'It's two o'clock, dear. I've brought you a cup of coffee.' He held the cup to her lips as though she were a child and she drank gratefully, feeling the heat spread through her sleep-numbed body. Then she rose to her feet. 'I'm all right now,' she said. 'Anything happened?'

'No. It's very quiet. Most of them are nervously as well as physically exhausted.' He held the pew door open for her and she went out. Maxl pattered behind, his tail and ears swinging like a Highlander's kilt.

Bill said, 'I'm going to sit with Mrs. Ventress for a while. Tom's beginning to come to a little and she's scared stiff. He's a bit delirious yet.'

'All right.'

Sue had a few casual whispered words with Kit, who presently vanished into a pew. Then there were rounds to make. Everyone was quiet, however, and there was little do except keep a general eye on the patients. Sue wondered where Marianna had gone and tried to realize that it was only the morning before that they had set out for the Pow farm. It seemed years ago. She moved slowly up to the front of the church and sat down on the steps below the chancel.

'I'm more tired than I realized,' she thought, 'and I can see everybody from here.' Maxl clambered up beside her and they sat together looking out over the shadowy honeycomb of pews, hearing the sound of many people breathing, the occasional thump as a knee or elbow struck a pew back, the whimper of a child and the murmured response of its mother. The rain had stopped entirely now. Someone had said that the lake would go down in about a week – maybe less. There was a good outlet at the other end of the valley. And the roads would soon be cleared, too. The worst job would be to prevent an epidemic of sickness after the water had gone down. Wells would be drowned and the people must realize that water from them could not be used unless it was chlorinated. They would have to be persuaded not to use potatoes and apples without washing them in chlorinated water. They must be taught how to clean walls and floors so that there would be no danger of infection – again the chlorinated water must be used. But would they do it? Yes, Sue thought, they would. They had had one dose of an epidemic and they would listen to Bill and Lot Phinney.

A dim figure came across from the side of the church – Martha Edgett, thin and restless.

'I'll sit with ye a while,' she whispered.

A moment later a dark portly bulk rose from a rear pew and tiptoed up the aisle.

'May I join you?' said Mr. Todd.

'Sartin',' Martha said – and Sue's quick ear caught a note of happiness in the crisp voice.

Elias Todd sat down on the bottom step, grunting a little, and reached out to pull Maxl's ears. The three sat without speaking for a time. Sue's blue uniform, stained and crumpled, made a splotch of colour against the carpeted steps. Martha Edgett's woollen dress melted into the darkness, but her face glimmered palely, and the dark shadow that was Elias Todd was turned towards it. Bill had moved out of the Ventress pew and was drifting here and there, bending down, straightening up – the only visible movement.

Mr. Todd cleared his throat.

'I'm glad your home will be untouched, Mrs. Edgett,' he said.

'So'm I.'

'This has been a most unfortunate occurrence. I – I hope I – er – have been of some help to you. If I could –'

'Ye've done fine fer us all, Mr. Todd.'

'Er – well, I've done my best. But I'd hoped that *you* –' He floundered, cleared his throat again, and fell silent. Sue came to his rescue.

'You've been marvellous, Mr. Todd! I don't know what we'd have done without you – do you, Mrs. Edgett?'

'He's been a help,' Martha admitted, and Sue, enchanted with this flowering of elderly romance, could have shaken her. Mr. Todd gazed at the thin face above him with admiring and hopeful eyes. The thin face gazed calmly out over the pews. Martha was not going to be moved by self-advertising, first or second-hand. Mr. Todd drew a deep breath and tried a different method.

'Miss Barton,' he said, trying to sound important, 'I've been wanting to – er – tell you for a long time –I – I have been very much impressed with the work you and the doctor have been doing – especially with – er – your efforts in the typhoid epidemic.'

Sue glanced at him sharply. He did know, then! That *was* why he had given her Maxl!

'I think the credit for that goes to Dr. Barry,' said Sue clearly.

'Oh – er – yes, of course, of course.' He paused, his eyes on Martha Edgett. 'Very commendable,' he said.

'What ye talkin' about?' said Martha abruptly. 'Land sakes! The doctor's as smart a young feller as ever we had in these parts! Commendable! He'd oughter have sumpthin' besides commendin'!'

'Oh yes, certainly. I'd be very glad to do anything for *you* – a little gift perhaps?'

'Gift!' Martha snorted. Then she leaned forward. 'Sue, ain't that Tom Ventress a movin' down there?'

Sue sprang up and ran down the steps. In the pew below Mrs. Ventress heaved uneasily. 'That'll hold it, boys,' Tom said.

Sue bent over him. 'He's coming along, Mrs. Ventress, don't worry. A blow on the head really can jar people right out of their senses, you know, and it takes a while to get back.'

'He's a good man, Miss Barton.'

'I know.' Sue's hand tightened on the vast shoulder. 'Can I get you anything, Mrs. Ventress?'

'No, thanks. I'm all right.'

As Sue tiptoed away she saw two backs, one a narrow ramrod, the other broad and thick-set, going rapidly down the aisle towards the front vestibule.

'Well!' said Sue under her breath.

'I hope to tell you!' said Bill, looming beside her. 'What goes on with those two?'

Sue's dimple was a sudden shadow in her cheek. 'Just what you think is going on *is* going on. Elias has been knocked down by an apron string and he likes it.'

'Are you sure? What about Martha?'

'Martha, too. It sticks out all over her – but she's being as difficult as she can. He's going to have to earn her.'

'Well, I'll be –' Bill grinned broadly. 'Think he'll pull it off?'

Laughter brimmed in Sue's eyes. 'Certainly he will! He just doesn't know it yet – and he's trying awfully hard. I think he yearns to do something terrific – just to show her. It's sweet!'

'Life begins at fifty! How'd you like to make a few rounds with me?'

'Wouldn't one be enough?'

'No.'

They moved away, stopping to look at sprawled figures, tucking in a blanket here, pausing there to feel a pulse. In the last pew on the side aisle they found Marianna and Freddie, side by side and both asleep. Freddie leaned against the wall, an arm protectively around Marianna, whose tousled hair rested against his shoulder.

Maxl scrabbled at the pew door and Sue pushed him back gently with her foot.

Marianna stirred.

'Sue?' she murmured without opening her eyes.

'Yes, lamb. What is it?' Sue leaned over the pew back.

'Sue – I – mm – I wanted to tell ya – this morning' – but I – got fussed. Sue, I'm – gonna stay an' be a nurse. You glad?'

'Yes, honey, *very*!'

'Mm. I'm gonna be an air hostess, Sue. Freddie says maybe – we can get on – the same ' Her voiced trailed off.

'Well!' Sue whispered for the second time. 'No, Maxl!' As they went away she murmured, 'We're wrong, Bill. This is no temporary hospital – this is a matrimonial agency!'

'You're telling me! You're relieved about the kid, aren't you?'

'I certainly am! Golly! So this summer's effort wasn't wasted after all! Though I will say that Freddie seems to have had a large share in changing her mind.'

'I don't think so,' Bill said seriously. 'Freddie helped, but Veazie Ann says that Marianna had been working up to it for a long time, she's sure. The kid couldn't quite bring herself to come out with it, that's all.'

'I know. She loathes giving in about anything.'

They continued on round the church, Maxl a hurrying little sausage at their heels.

'Look, Bill,' said Sue, coming out of her pleased preoccupation with Marianna, 'it's going to be daylight in a minute.'

'Sure enough. Oh Lord! They're starting to wake up! I wish they'd slept a little longer. It's going to make a long day of it.'

There was a stir all over the church. Heads appeared in pews. Rumpled figures rose against the grey oblongs of the windows. Kit sat up in her corner and stretched. Lot Phinney appeared out of nowhere, limping and tired. Ira Prouty materialized with Veazie Ann and both made for the stove. Marianna and Freddie, stiff but bright-eyed with the resilience of youth, hobbled out of their pew. Children began to scamper in the aisles, pursued by grabbing mothers. Outside the trees lifted battered branches to a clear sky that grew brighter moment by moment.

Bill paused to bend over George.

'He might have a taste of whisky and milk, Sue.'

George's face had a better colour but it was still too grey. He drank a little of the whisky and milk that Sue brought and then pushed the cup away. 'I don't want no more right now,' he said. 'Jest leave the cup on th' floor. I'll take another swallow pretty soon.'

Sue put the cup down and turned to speak to Bill. She didn't see Maxl approach the cup with intent eyes – but George did, and brightened. He made no move to stop Maxl, whose pink tongue came out and dipped into the cup, lapping steadily until the last drop was finished.

Martha Edgett and Elias Todd came in from the vestibule and crossed at once to Sue and Bill.

'Go on, Mr. Todd,' said Martha. 'Tell him!'

Elias cleared his throat. 'I – er –' he began, and looked at Martha. She nodded violently. 'I – Doctor, would it be – could you – er –'

'*Sakes alive!*' Martha exclaimed. 'Dr. Barry, Mr. Todd wants to give th' town a little hospital.'

'*What?*' said Bill, suddenly pale. Sue gasped.

'A hospital!' Martha said. 'He feels it would be a good thing for everybody – and land knows, he's had trouble enough with sick folks up at his place to make it wuth his while fer that alone. The nerve of that man, a tryin' to sue him! An' as I told him, th' town needs it. And he'd like to do sumpthin' for you.'

Elias found his voice at last. 'I'd like to put you in charge of it. I've been impressed with your capability in this emergency, Doctor, and I feel that I won't be making a mistake.' He turned to the stunned and incredulous Sue. 'Mrs. Edgett,' he said, 'considers that a small training school would be a fine thing for the young girls in the vicinity. Fifteen or twenty students, I should think. We'd like you to take charge of that, Miss Barton. Oh – and Mrs. Edgett has offered a tract of her land for a site, and –'

'Whoopee!' said Marianna.

A rising murmur of approval and excitement rose from the pews. The townspeople crowded round Elias. Martha Edgett, openly proud and admiring at last, was at his side.

It was Elias Todd's hour.

Sue touched Bill on the arm. 'Let's go outside,' she whispered, 'and watch the sunrise.'

Bill followed her out to the steps, but neither of them looked at the sunrise. They looked at each other, unaware of the mists smoking up out of a drowned valley below, for they were very tired, very young – and their dream had come true. They saw only the brick wall and white trimness of their little hospital rising before them – its sunny wards, its operating-room, its clinic, its X-ray machines.

'Dr. William Barry, Superintendent of the Springdale Hospital,' Sue murmured.

'*And* Miss Sue Barton, Superintendent of Nurses!'

Their hands went out to each other in wordless happiness. Speech wasn't necessary. They knew that Kit would be Sue's assistant, that Bill would have an interne, perhaps two, to take the burden of night work from his shoulders. They knew that Marianna would train there.

Sue thought of her own student days. Her nurses would do the same things, she knew – they would be out after hours and climb in windows, they would get into scrapes, they would fall in love with the interne. Marianna could raise Cain. And Sue would be responsible for them all, separately and collectively.

She said aloud. 'It – it's preposterous, Bill! I – a Superintendent of Nurses!'

'You'll be a peach, darling. I suppose it will take a year or two to build, don't you?'

'I wouldn't know. Does it matter?'

'No!'

'We'll have our Welfare Clinic, and our Maternity Centre, and –'

'*Good God!*' Lot Phinney's old voice rang out from the doorway. '*Look at the valley!*'

There, below, the roofs of Springdale stood like grey tents on a silver field, the mists curling round them. Beyond, clouds slept in the folds of the mountains. No breath of wind stirred. No ripple moved in the water. The mountains were mirrored crystal clear in Main Street.

One by one the people of Springdale – all who were quick on their feet still – came out and down the church steps, moving silently to the edge of the cliff. Many were bandaged. All were pale, and their eyes, which had been so cheerful half an hour ago, were full with the shock of realization. They had forgotten – because they hadn't really believed. Now they saw that it was true.

In the long silence they gazed downwards, not moving. Then, as Sue watched, aching with sympathy, thin-lipped New England mouths tightened; lean jaws set forward; shoulders squared. The women straightened tired backs; their eyes cleared with purpose; worn hands steadied, smoothing rumpled aprons. Somebody drew a long breath – but before anyone could speak, a hiccough dropped into the stillness like a pebble into a pool.

Heads turned towards the sound and startled eyes beheld an incredible and ridiculous sight.

Maxl stood on the top step, long, low, and leering. He swayed, and hiccoughed again. The little jerk propelled him forwards and he reeled down the steps, his mouth open and his tongue lolling in a gigantic, hilarious grin.

'By golly,' Lot Phinney cried, 'th' little cuss is *drunk*!'

Maxl continued on his way, stepping high over pebbles, his scythe-like tail flourishing ribald cheer. '*Ip!*' he said, and again '*Ip!*' In the centre of the half-circle of staring human beings he collapsed like a deflated balloon and sprawled, a grinning black-and-tan heap. '*Ip!*' he said, and his tail beat a tattoo on the gravel at his own joke.

The silence was broken by a spontaneous crash of laughter. The people of Springdale shouted, caught their breaths, choked, and shouted again. Other faces appeared in the doorway, stared, and crumpled into mirth. Tears ran down cheeks to which the colour was returning for the first time in many hours. 'I gorry!' they cried, and wiped streaming eyes.

The hills caught their laughter and flung it back. It rang out over the drowned valley and returned in hearty roars as the first sunlight poured down the blue mountain slopes.

Lot Phinney's voice, quivering but strong, came from somewhere behind Sue.

'Looks like it's a goin' to be a good day, folks!'